From Hate to Love

From **Hate** to **Love**

a survivor's story

ROBERT SAUNDERS

BOOK WRITER PRESS

ISBN-10: 0692424466
ISBN-13: 978-0692424469

Contents

Forward

Robert Saunders is a true miracle of God. I am also proud to call him my husband and best friend. Robert writes with such passion that it spills out of nearly every word on the page.

The book you hold in your hand is an awesome testament to the power of God. This story was written from a prison cell by a man who found true freedom. It is the story of a tragic and traumatic childhood and a God who heals beyond belief. This story is based on Robert's life experience, though not exactly true to life to protect a certain number of people.

Thank you for taking the time to read this book, and it is my prayer that somehow you will see the awesomeness of God and draw you closer to Him.

Be blessed,
Jackie Saunders

One

Lost Innocence

As the storm rolled in the sky grew quickly dark. First came the lightening; then the thunder seemed to shake the whole house. That's the part that always scared Tina the most.

It was early September and Adam and Tina, 10 and 6, were once again home alone.

Over the last couple of months their single mom was rarely home at night. Adam still remembered her words, "Adam, you know, now that your daddy is gone you will have to be the man of the house and take care of your sister. Your daddy did this, not me. He is a low down snake."

Adam could remember the many fights his mom and dad had and how Tina always ran to his room to hide. Both of them, scared and shaking, would hide in his closet until the last door slammed and the house was quiet again. Even now a thunderstorm reminded him of the slamming doors.

It reminded Tina too. She ran to Adam to hold her and keep her safe.

"Oh great! What am I going to do now? I'm only ten," Adam thought to himself. "How can I do anything for Tina or me? But he couldn't let Tina see him cry; that would really upset her and he didn't want her more upset than she was.

Adam cleared his voice, choked back his tears and said, "Tina, don't cry. You don't need to be scared, I'll protect you. It's only a thunderstorm anyway."

Adam put a frozen pizza in the oven, along with some French fries – the crinkly kind that Tina loved so much. This was the fifth night in a row that they ate frozen pizza but as long as he did something a little different each time Tina didn't seem to notice. Or if she did, she never let on.

"I wonder," thought Adam, "why Tina doesn't ask questions, like – 'Where's momma?' or 'Why hasn't daddy been back?' 'Why do we have to eat pizza every night?'…Maybe she's too young or maybe she doesn't care." Adam just sighed and took a small bit of the already cold pizza.

"Tina, we have school in the morning so you need to hurry and eat."

"What day is tomorrow?" asked Tina.

"Monday," replied Adam.

"Oh goody! Ms. Sherry said she would bring homemade cookies for our snack. She is the teacher's aide. She said someday she will be a teacher just like Ms. Jet. When is momma coming home?" Tina asked, barely taking a breath between sentences.

"I, uhmmm…not sure," Adam said. "I think she must have had to work late."

Adam didn't like lying to Tina but he didn't

know what else to say. He threw the note away that he found on the kitchen counter that morning after he got up. Adam could say it by memory – every note was the same. "Adam, remember you're the man of the house now. So take care of your sister. I'll be home late. There is food in the fridge. Love, Mom."

"Love, Mom!" shouted Adam silently in his head. "If she loved us how could she stay gone all the time?!"

Adam couldn't show Tina he was upset. So he stuffed his anger deep into his gut.

"Tina, please go get ready for bed and I'll take care of the dishes. And don't forget to brush your teeth," Adam yelled down the hall to Tina.

By the time Adam had the dishes done and the garbage emptied Tina appeared in the kitchen with her stuffed pink bunny clinched in her arms. "I'm ready to go to sleep now. Will you check for monsters in the closet?"

"Yeah, sure," said Adam. "But you know, Tina, monsters don't live in your closet."

"How do you know Adam?"

"Because…have we ever found one?"

"No, I guess not," said Tina.

"See, no monsters then."

"Adam," said Tina as she was crawling into bed, "when Momma gets home don't forget to tell her to come in here and say goodnight, okay?"

"Okay," replied Adam.

"You promise?"

"Yep, you bet I promise." Adam really hated to tell Tina he would do it because most nights he didn't know when his Mom would come home. Sometimes he only knew the next morning because of the cigarette butts in the ashtray.

Adam left Tina's room and went to the couch in the small living room. He looked around at the few pieces of furniture...large green couch, an orange love seat, and a brown bean bag was all there was to sit on. The T.V. sat on a wobbly table, and most of the time it didn't work anyway. So Adam laid back and turned on his white transistor radio. Adam loved to listen to the music. Adam would daydream about being a singer. They seemed so happy and lots of people liked them. This is where Adam would hide his emotions, in a fantasy land.

Tonight was too much, though. With his Mom gone since before they woke up, and still not home as they were going to bed, Adam began to cry. He didn't understand what was happening to him, but he knew he was scared and all alone. He cried even harder.

Adam woke to the sun beaming through his bedroom window and the birds singing in the old maple tree outside. Adam suddenly realized that he was in his own bed – "Momma," he said as he ran down the hall to her bedroom. He quietly approached and noticed the door was somewhat ajar. Peering in, not sure what he would find, he was relieved to see that his Momma was alone in bed. Many mornings he had heard strange men's voices coming from the bedroom, or walking by the kitchen table as he and Tina ate breakfast. Breakfast was almost always corn flakes and watered down milk. Momma always told them, "Milk is expensive and your Daddy's child support is late again."

Pushing the door open gently, he said, "Momma, you awake?" With no reply he stepped closer to the bed. "Momma? You awake?" A soft unintelligible mumble came from his Momma whose face was buried deep in her pillow. Adam moved even closer, "Momma?" As she moved around trying to find a more comfortable position, he caught a whiff of booze and stale cigarette smoke – an all too familiar odor.

"Drunk again," Adam said to himself. He knew it wouldn't do any good to wake her; she wouldn't remember anyway. With the familiar command of "Adam, you have to be the man of the house now…" playing in his mind he left the room to get Tina up, fed, and on the bus to school.

Adam didn't ride the bus much anymore. He like the mile and a half walk because it helped him to clear his head before classes started.

Adam was struggling with most of his classes. When the teachers asked to see his Momma he always covered for her – "Ms. Jones, you know my Momma is really busy working these days…You know, ever since Daddy left, she's been workin' two jobs." Adam sure didn't want to lie, but if they found out the truth, it would be horrible for Tina and him. He heard about how the state would come and take them away, and split he and Tina up. Adam had convinced himself he would never tell the truth and risk that.

Adam didn't really like school but he remembered what Mr. Horton, his fifth grade math teacher, always said – "Good grades means a good job." The teachers knew that Adam was smart; he just didn't apply himself to his work.

Adam thought to himself, "Report cards are coming up soon. I better try a little harder to raise my grades. I sure don't need the teachers comin' to the house or sending the police."

With fall break six weeks away Adam felt confident he could at least get his D's to C's. Surely that would take the heat off. As Adam thought more about school he began to realize that he really felt safe – especially with teachers like Mrs. V.

Adam was the thin and wiry type, with blonde hair and hazel eyes. Adam and Tina were only in their second year at Washington Elementary. Neither of them had many friends. And as was typical, the quiet-shy types got a lot of harassment from the bullies. One day after school six boys grabbed Adam and tied him to the schoolyard fence and left him there. If it wasn't for a couple of brave sixth graders, who knows how long Adam would have been there.

Adam tried very hard to hide his feelings, but he had had enough. There he sat in front of Ms. Jones office. Usually Ms. Jones, the principal, would smile and say "hello", but not this time. She scowled and tapped her pen as she waited for Adam's mom to answer the phone. She needed to explain to Adam's mother about the discipline required for fighting. Adam had punched Joey in the face and made his nose bleed.

Adam sat in the big chair in front of Ms. Jones' desk with a thousand thoughts racing through his mind. "Boy, mamma will probably beat me again," thought Adam. Adam had never hit anyone – that he could remember…if forgetting to clean up the kitchen got you a beatin' from momma, this would be really bad!"

Some moments went by and Ms. Jones gave up on the phone call. "Young man! I am very disappointed in you."

"Yes, ma'am," came a quivering response from Adam.

"I see from your school records that you have never been in trouble."

"Yes ma'am. I mean, no ma'am, I haven't," said Adam.

"Well, then what do you think we ought to do about this mess?" asked Ms. Jones.

Puzzled by the question, Adam's only response was a shocked, "Huh?," not believing that he would have any say in the matter.

"What do you think should be your punishment?"

"Uhmm, I could sit in here with you every recess for a week."

Ms. Jones smiled and started to chuckle. She had never heard that one in twenty years of teaching. "Well Adam, that is quite an offer. I will give you two recesses in here with me, and please don't let it happen again. I don't like handing out punishments," replied Ms. Jones.

"Yes ma'am," agreed Adam.

"Whew! What a relief. Momma will never know now," Adam said to himself on his way back to class. This confirmed even more to Adam that school was okay. Adam resolved in himself to get really good grades. Maybe that would make him feel better and maybe then people would like him.

In no time at all both his spelling and math skills began to advance. Fall soon turned into winter, but nothing changed at home. Momma stayed gone while Adam earned extra money shoveling snow. Holidays were non-existent. After the Christmas break Adam avoided every conversation about the gifts each one received. One gift that Adam was proud of was the new doll he bought for Tina. Most of the money he earned was used to buy milk and bread when momma forgot. Ten year olds didn't make much money shoveling snow. "Maybe when I turn eleven I'll make more," Adam thought to himself.

But Adam wouldn't be eleven until July 7th. That's summertime, which meant no school and no one to take care of Tina while he was off trying to find odd jobs. Well, Tina would be seven on April 22nd. Maybe she could tag along - at least he would know she was alright that way.

Tina had become Adam's whole life. He had been protecting her since she was two years old. Many times Adam hid Tina and himself in his bedroom closet while his parents fought or had wild parties. Adam was committed to protecting Tina, and never once did he consider it a burden. He loved her, and she loved him.

Adam knew he had to stay busy. To stop to think about all that was happening to them would crush him, and would only cause more problems for Tina.

Winter became spring and Adam noticed that the beatings by his momma had stopped. He guessed that was because she was gone so much, but he wasn't sure which was worse — beatings or abandonment. Either way, no one could ever find out about it, or they would split up Tina and Adam for sure!

Adam was committed to being a loner and told Tina the same thing. "Tina, we can't have friends over to the house."

"Why not?" asked Tina.

"Cause if people find out momma ain't around much they will call the police," replied Adam.

"What does that mean, Adam?"

"Well, they will come get us and split us up."

"Split us up? What do you mean?" Tina asked.

"You would have to live somewhere with strangers, and they would make me live in a different place, with strangers. We wouldn't be together anymore."

Tina became scared and started to cry, "Adam, don't let them take me away!"

"I won't, I won't," Adam said as he grabbed a hold of Tina. "Everything is going to be okay. I promise!" Adam committed himself to that promise with tears in his eyes and teeth clinched with anger.

"Tina, it's getting late. You need to be up for school in the morning. It's the last day for the whole week."

"Yeah!" said Tina. "Then the next day is my birthday!"

"Yep. You will be seven years old. I guess you are growing up fast, huh?"

"Yep, I sure am!" said Tina, smiling as she headed down the hall.

"Don't forget to brush your teeth!" yelled Adam.

"I won't" came her reply.

Adam sat at the old wooden table where they ate their meals and spread out his homework. Tests were coming up and he wanted to do good – that way Mrs. V. would be happy with him. Mr. Horton would always tell him, "Keep it up, son, and you can get a really good job when you are older."

In no time at all, Tina was back. "Adam," Tina said, "I am ready for bed…but you don't need to check for monsters. I'm a big girl now."

"Okay," said Adam, kind of stunned. "Good night then."

With that, she was off like a flash.

Two things bothered Adam at that moment. Tina was growing up too fast and, like him, would she even know what it was like to just be a kid? That, and the fact that she had stopped reminding him to tell momma to come say goodnight to her.

Adam thought really hard about these things and wondered if he was being selfish. Maybe if the police did split them up, Tina would get a new family where she could just be a kid for a while. Shocked by his own thoughts, he said, "You're lying to yourself, Adam. Those people are just like momma and daddy. They don't like kids. Forget it."

He accepted that thought and went to work on his science homework.

Adam fell asleep at the table and was startled by voices and laughter he heard coming from the front of the house. Half awake he squinted to see the old clock on the wall. It was 1am. The door opened and his momma staggered into the house giggling like a school girl, while some strange man had his hands all over her.

Adam froze in fear of what momma would do to him. He often remembered the middle-of-the-night beatings. He was blamed for the babysitter quitting. It wasn't his fault, like they claimed. It was his daddy's fault. Daddy would come home when the babysitter was there. They were always high school juniors or seniors and he would mess with them, trying to grab them. Daddy would say things like, "Boy, women ain't good for nothin' but sex. You will learn that someday, maybe." When he didn't get what he wanted, he left. If those girls ever told momma, she didn't care. And Adam got the beating.

"Maybe if I just sit here real quiet, she won't notice me," Adam thought.

The man stopped and looked right at Adam. "Hey kid, you up kinda late, ain't ya?"

Adam's mouth went dry and his palm began to sweat. "I…fell asleep," Adam said through a cracked voice.

"Boy, you better get to bed now!" his momma thundered.

"Yes, ma'am," Adam ran to his bedroom. Shaking like a leaf, Adam hid under his covers and worried about what would come next…belt, a hand, or a piece of wood. He had felt all of them at one time or another.

2am rolled around and Adam finally fell asleep, exhausted from fear. When Adam woke up, he checked to see if there was a strange car in the driveway. There wasn't; just mamma's car. Had there ever been two cars? Was last night just a dream?

Adam couldn't tell. He wondered if the man was still there. He wasn't like most of the men, though. He was clean and well dressed, like a businessman would be. He was not the kind of men momma normally hung around.

Adam, as usual, checked to see if momma was alone or awake before he woke Tina. The door to the bedroom was wide open and mamma was alone. As he stepped into the room a pile of twenty dollar bills on the dresser caught his eye. There must have been ten of them! Adam had never seen that much money at one time before. He was quite familiar with welfare checks and food stamps. He didn't know what to think and quietly backed out of the room, pulling the door closed as he left.

On the way to school Adam thought about how to get his birthday present for Tina. The gift was going to be a yellow ribbon for her hair. Yellow was Tina's favorite color, Adam recalled. He let himself smile at the thought of how excited Tina would be to get it.

The ribbon idea first came to him when he saw Sue wearing one in her hair. Sue was Adam's heartthrob. Of course, no one knew that but Adam. Sue sat in front of him in math class. She was kinda short, had beautiful blonde hair and really blue eyes. Although she was friendly and all, Adam just wasn't in her league. Her daddy must have made a lot of money because she wore name brand clothes and nail polish. At least twice a week she wore a yellow ribbon in her hair.

Adam was so shy around Sue. He would avoid her instead of embarrassing himself in front of her by stumbling over his words. However, Tina was more important than his pride.

"Sue, uhmm…can I ask you a question?" Adam couldn't believe how he had opened his mouth and the words had just fallen out.

Sue turned to face Adam; His face turned red and he started to sweat.

"Yes, Adam," replied Sue. Her voice sounded like a chorus of angels.

Adam stood paralyzed.

"Adam, what is the question?" Sue asked.

With a pause, Adam said, "Tomorrow is my little sister's birthday and she will be seven. Yellow is her favorite color and I want to buy her a yellow ribbon for her hair, and, so…where did you get yours?"

Before Sue could answer Adam nervously blurted out, "I have money. I can buy it myself!"

Sue reached back in her hair and let the yellow ribbon loose. Shaking out her hair, she handed the ribbon to Adam and said, "I don't think my brother would do that for me, so I will give you mine and you can give it to your sister as a gift from yourself. Keep your money for something else."

If Sue knew Adam's home life, she never let on or embarrassed him with it.

Adam very politely said, "Thank you. It will mean a lot to her."

He carefully folded it up and put it in his pocket. Adam remembered the wrapping paper he was going to use – it came from a trashcan on his route to school. Pink balloons with the phrase "Happy Birthday" written in yellow letters. He had hidden it in his sock drawer so no one could see it. Everything had to be a surprise.

Adam devoted most of the day to paying attention in class. School had become Adam's only escape from life. He often wondered if it would be the same for Tina.

As Adam walked home from school he usually worried about what he would find when he got home, but today was different. Today his thoughts were on whether or not momma would miss another birthday. She missed both of their birthdays last year. How does a momma forget giving birth to a baby? Mrs. V. said that it is a momma's gift each year to remember her babies being born.

Adam walked through the door of their house about thirty minutes before Tina got home. "Momma!" yelled Adam. "Momma! You here?"

An all too familiar silence echoed back. Leaning back against the door, he looked around. He saw dust particles floating in the air as the late afternoon sun shone through the smoke filmed window bordered by old dusty drapes. The odor of stale smoke still

15

hung in the air.

The silence gripped his heart as he slid down the door in a huddled mass on the floor. He cried, and cried bitterly. "Am I going crazy?" he wondered. "Is this what it's like to be crazy?…How could I take care of Tina if I was crazy??" With those thoughts he stuffed his feelings deep inside – "Tina can't see me like this."

Adam was exhausted from it all but he pulled himself up and made his way to the kitchen. His thoughts turned to Tina and the snack he needed to prepare for her. He was too emotionally drained to even react to the words of the note.

"Adam, remember you're the man of the house now, so take care of your sister."

As he read the rest of the note he was determined to not cry or feel anything, but he couldn't help himself. The tears that fell from his face landed on the note.

"Stay in the house and no friends. I will be back late Sunday. You know I've got to work. The money is to buy food down at the store. Mom."

Adam stood at the counter and stared at the note in total disbelief. "How could she?" Adam thought to himself. "How could she!!" he screamed out loud, not realizing that at that moment Tina walked through the door and heard him.

"How could she what?" asked Tina, now standing in the doorway of the kitchen.

"Tina!" exclaimed Adam. Startled he turned to face her.

"How could she what, Adam?" repeated Tina.

"Oh, no big deal. Momma forgot something at the store," said Adam quickly and casually, as he grabbed up the note and money and shoved them deep into his jeans pocket.

"Hey Tina, let's go to the store and pick out your favorite food. Maybe they'll have those chocolate cupcakes you love so much."

"Yeah!" shouted Tina. "Can we go now?"

"Yep, let's go now," Adam said, relieved that the questions about momma had ended. He still wasn't sure how to handle Tina's birthday, though.

Adam and Tina worked late into the night on a three hundred and fifty piece puzzle of the Chicago skyline. Adam had found it in the discount basket for $1.50 and thought it would kill some time. Sure enough, it did. By 11pm Tina was falling asleep at the table. Adam picked Tina up and carried her to bed, turned off her light, and went back to the living room.

To avoid thinking about the note Adam turned on his transistor radio and listened to WLS out of Chicago. He had never seen a big city in person. Now the puzzle gave him a picture of one of the biggest cities in the whole country. Having never been out of this small rural town in central Illinois, Chicago sure looked exciting. It captured the dreams of this young boy and lifted them as high as the skyscrapers. He started listening to all the radio ads that promised a future to anyone and day dreamed about going there someday. For the first time in weeks, Adam fell asleep without crying.

Waking up still on the couch, Adam went through the morning ritual. He checked to see if his mother was home before waking up Tina. He was hurt, but not surprised, that she was not there. In another feeble attempt to make himself feel better, he thought to himself, "At least she didn't say she would be here and wasn't."

Adam mustered up the strength to plan a great day for Tina's birthday. He wrapped the ribbon up in the wrapping paper he had found and positioned the pink balloons just right with "Happy Birthday" written in yellow letters.

"Tina's Day!" announced Adam as he woke her up.

She smiled and yelled, "Yay! I'm seven now!" The smell of French toast sticks made her stomach growl as they headed to the breakfast table.

Adam watched his sister dip her sticks in warm syrup and smile with each bit. "So innocent," he thought. "What will happen when she catches on and realizes what is going on in our family?" If he could help it, it wouldn't happen today.

Adam shook off the chill that ran down his spine and offered a game of "hid-and-seek" to Tina. He allowed the game to go outside as well, but only in their yard. Who would see them anyway? Their nearest neighbor was half a mile away and there were trees that blocked the view - except in the winter. When the leaves were gone, you could see if the house lights were on.

After hours of fun - running, hiding, jumping rope, and picking dandelions, the two of them were exhausted. Naps were still something Tina enjoyed but Adam thought he was too old and had too much to do.

Adam planned to surprise Tina with the prized yellow ribbon at dinner. Tina was the princess and he was the servant.

"Dinner at six, my lady," Adam announced in his best British accent.

Tina giggled saying she would wear her favorite yellow dress and went off to take her nap.

Adam relaxed for a little while and thought of every detail to make this dinner just right. The menu was chicken tenders, crinkle cut fries, pre-made jello and Kool-Aid. Dessert included chocolate cupcakes with chocolate icing.

Promptly at 6pm, Adam again mustered up a British accent saying, "Dinner is served, my lady!"

Tina replied, "Thank you, my servant," and laughed. Even Adam chuckled at her response.

Adam served the cupcakes on a round cookie tray as though it was a silver platter. "Dessert, madam?" Adam offered.

"Thank you, servant," She responded. Both broke out laughing. Cold milk – and not watered down either – washed down the chocolate cupcakes.

"Here Tina," Adam said as he handed her the wrapped package. "Just a little something I thought you might like."

"What is it?" asked Tina.

"Open and see," said Adam.

"Wow, Adam! It's a yellow ribbon! My favorite color, too!" Tina shouted excitedly. Adam was amazed at how well it matched Tina's yellow dress. "Help me tie it, Adam."

Adam tied the ribbon in a bow just like Sue did. "There you go." With that, Tina bolted for the bathroom mirror to get a good look.

"Adam, it's so pretty. I love it! Thank you."

"Yeah, you're welcome."

The rest of the day was spent finishing the puzzle and cleaning up the kitchen.

"It worked," Adam said to himself as he crawled onto the couch to listen to the radio. "Tina's day worked."

It was Sunday afternoon when momma came home. She had two arms full of groceries and pretended as though she were only gone a few hours at the store instead of three days to who knows where. Adam was skeptical but Tina was excited because she hadn't seen momma in over a week.

Adam hung back while his momma put on a

show as though she loved and cared for them. She handed out candy and little trinkets. Adam wondered if his momma's display was for real and how long it would last. Adam knew better than to ask too many questions and didn't want to spoil the time Tina was having.

Tina carried on like nothing was wrong. She told her momma about school, the friends she had there, and all the neat things she was learning.

After a few hours momma rushed Tina off to do her homework and get ready for bed. "You have school tomorrow, you know," Momma reminded her.

"Yes, momma," came Tina's response, and off she went.

Momma turned to Adam, "Adam, I want to see you in my room."

"Yes, ma'am," Adam replied.

He stood at the foot of the bed, frozen like a soldier in front of a commanding officer. His momma lit a cigarette, took a long drag, and let it out. She began lecturing him about being responsible and told him that someday he would appreciate what she was doing for him. Adam's mind and emotions swirled around. He tried to understand what she was saying, but nothing made sense. It was all he could do to stare and say, "Yes, ma'am."

All Adam wanted from his momma was a hug and to be loved. Adam stood there and wondered what he did to make his momma hate him so much.

He quickly shoved that thought away. To accidentally blurt it out would surely result in a beating. Momma finished lecturing and said to Adam, "You're excused. Go check on your sister. I need to be alone."

With that, Adam turned and walked out.

Two

A Little Too Little Too Late

The last month of school whizzed by for Adam. Keeping up with his grades, mowing the lawn, and taking care of Tina left little time to contemplate his own needs – not that anyone would, or could, accuse him of being selfish. He was only ten and needed love and hugs like any child. Adam never complained. He mostly believed that no one would care anyway. His daddy taught him, "Boy, if you're gonna make it in this world, you got to make it on your own."

Adam was very pleased with his final report card. His social studies and science grades were average, while his spelling and math grades were both above average. Mrs. V. was also very proud and congratulated Adam for a job well done. He knew his momma wouldn't care – even if he had to re-do fifth grade three or four times, she wouldn't care. So there was no point in telling her the good news. Besides, now that school was over, he needed to get busy finding odd jobs. The money would really help, and so would being busy.

Adam needed a plan. He knew it took about

forty minutes to walk the mile and a half to school. If he pulled Tina along in a wagon, it would probably take about fifty minutes. With the nearest house half a mile away he would need to get started by 7:30 a.m. There were plenty of houses after that first one. Adam was willing to work hard and do a good job. He remembered the promise he made to Tina to always take care of her, no matter what.

Business came pretty easy for Adam. It seemed as though he was a natural salesman. He and Tina made a great team, too. They weeded flower beds, washed cars, cut grass, washed windows…and one customer hired them to wash her dog until the cast on her foot could come off. Most people paid more than the asking wage. Before June was over they had a mile worth of customers and never a dull moment.

At home, everything remained the same, with momma being gone most of the time. If she knew about them leaving every day, she didn't let on. Adam was determined to keep going even if he got beaten for it. He had promised to take care of Tina no matter what.

The air hung heavy and hot as the two made their way down the road. The morning of July 7th had come so fast. The temperature was already eighty degrees at 7:30! The high was to be 100. Adam and Tina had begun sweating only five minutes into their walk to scrounge for work.

The draught that started mid-June had taken a

toll on their business. With the water ban in effect the grass they once mowed was burning up. "Can't wash cars either," thought Adam. Even the once resilient weeds were giving up. According to the news reports, most of July would be the same. "And this is my birthday," Adam thought to himself. "I'm eleven now. Soon I will be old enough to leave home."

Adam was too busy focusing on the need to take care of Tina that he never mentioned his birthday, or stopped by the store to get himself anything.

Adam looked back to notice that Tina was falling behind. "Tina, you alright?

"Yeah, just hot I guess," Tina replied. Adam suggested they stop and sit in the shade for a bit.

After several minutes of silence, Tina asked, "Whatcha thinkin' bout, Adam?"

"Stuff."

"What kinda stuff, Adam?" Tina persisted.

"Ya know, work," said Adam. "We need work and not having rain has caused the grass not to grow," he added.

"You know, Adam…I wish we could work inside where it's cool!" proclaimed Tina. "Some people have air conditioning or something like that. Is that what they call it?" The words came out as fast as her little mind could think.

"Yeah, that's it. You're right, Tina," Adam said as he jumped to his feet. "I bet we could do inside chores. Why there's a bunch of things we could do!

Dust, vacuum, clean out closets. We even have a wagon to take away the stuff they don't want! You're really smart Tina," Adam told her as he offered her up.

"You think so, Adam?"

"Yep, I sure do. Why I bet you are the smartest kid I know – even though you are a girl," Adam added with a little snicker.

"Hey you," said Tina, punching him in the arm. "Take it back!"

"Okay, okay, I'm *just* kidding. You know I am."

"You better be," said Tina.

After five "not today kids" Adam and Tina finally struck gold. Mrs. Newsome was home. She was an older lady Adam reasoned, by her graying hair. Adam and Tina were hired for the whole day, and it was all inside work. They cleaned out closets, swept the basement, dusted furniture, vacuumed, cleaned out the cat litter box – "Yuck", Tina said at the smell – and other odds and ends.

Mrs. Newsom called it quits at 3pm. She had fed them lunch, gave them lemonade breaks, and commended them for a job well done. With that, she handed each of them $10.00 and sent them home pulling a wagon full of old toys and clothes that belonged to her children when they were young.

"Wow," Adam said quietly, "What a birthday after all."

Adam and Tina were so excited at all the neat

stuff they were given by Mrs. Newsom. They dumped the big black garbage bag full of stuff out on the living room floor. Tina found a red velvet dress with a real silk lining and black dress shoes. Adam found some old metal cards, an old cap pistol, and cowboy boots. They spent the whole evening trying on clothes and looking into the kaleidoscope they got.

After Tina had gone to bed, Adam laid back on the couch, turned on his radio, and began to day-dream about going to Chicago some day and making it big in business.

The next four weeks went by pretty quickly as the two stayed busy. The rain came mid-July and gave a brief relief to both the heat and the drought.

Adam and Tina had managed to earn and save enough money to buy three outfits each for the new school year. To Adam's surprise, momma came through with backpacks and school supplies.

Adam was excited about 6th grade. Mrs. V. would be his homeroom teacher and his Social Studies teacher. Not to mention, this would be his last year in elementary school. With his focus on both school and Tina, thoughts of anger and sorrow concerning momma's way of treating them remained stuffed deep inside.

It was mid-August and school started with a flurry. Adam and Tina were both excited and ready to learn as they got used to new classrooms and new kids.

While Adam started to come out of his quiet shell, Tina remained somewhat shy.

Tina was so happy to find out that Ms. Sherry was now her teacher. She came home and excitedly spilled out a bunch of stories from her day – "We had spelling in the morning, Ms. Sherry read from a book to us, we had some math to do – yuck – recess and lunch…"

"Slow down, slow down, Tina," interrupted Adam. "I can't even understand half of what you are saying!"

"Okay." Tina took a deep breath in, let it out, and then went on.

Adam laughed when Tina got to the point where Joey, who sits two desks behind her, asked if he could be her boyfriend.

"Ha ha! Hey – you're only in 3nd grade. Why would you want a boyfriend?" asked Adam.

"I told him 'No way!'" Tina said gruffly with her hands on her hips.

"Okay, okay, don't get huffy. I'm just kidding ya know."

"Well, he is nice to me anyway," Tina added quickly. "He smiles at me and he even said he would sit with me on the bus. I guess friends is okay, right Adam?"

"Sure thing. Have lots of friends!" Adam replied.

Adams concept of friends came from their customers. Neither of them knew what real friendship was like. With their parents split up, they didn't have any role models at home, and they were too far from the other kids from school. Not to mention the fact that they never knew when their momma would be home – they couldn't risk anyone coming to the house.

Weekdays were full of school and homework. Adam had become very persistent in doing his absolute best and making sure that Tina had the same attitude. Tina was too young to understand why school work was so important.

Adam had become angry and frustrated at Tina's apparent "no big deal attitude". He pounded his fist on the table and barked out, "If you're gonna make it in this world, you gotta make it on your own!"

With that Tina burst into tears and ran to her room.

Adam stood at the table all alone, shocked at what he had just done. A million "why's" ran through his head, "What have I done?" Then he heard Tina crying. "Oh no! Oh no! Tina!!" Adam said as he ran to Tina's door.

"Tina? Hey, it's Adam."

Tina replied through sobs and sniffles, "What? What do you want?"

"I'm sorry. I didn't mean to hurt your feelings. Can we talk?"

He heard Tina blow her nose, then she opened the door with her pink bunny in her arms, who was now soaked from her tears. Adam began to cry when he saw his little sister's swollen eyes and all the sadness that he caused her.

Tina gave Adam a hug and said, "Don't cry, Adam. I'm okay. I know you didn't mean it. You're the best brother anyone could have." Tina went on and repeated one of Adam's sayings, "We're a team, right? You said that we're the best team, right?"

"Yeah, you're right, Tina, and I promise not to ever yell at you again."

Later that night while he laid on the couch and listened to his radio, Adam's thoughts raced back to yelling at his sister. "What's happened to me?" Adam couldn't figure out why he would have done anything to hurt Tina. As hard as he tried, he couldn't keep from crying.

Angry, sad, confused, and uncertain about his and Tina's future, Adam cried himself to sleep.

• • • • •

Mid-October brought fall break. Joey and Nathan said they were going to Panama Beach. Sue and her family were going to her grandma's house in Daytona Beach. Sarah and Tommy were headed to the Bahama's on a cruise ship. All of them were going with their parents. Not once did Adam allow himself to envy his classmates or feel sorry for himself. He was going to make the best of the week off for Tina's sake.

Adam and Tina worked hard each day. One customer told her neighbor about the two children who cleaned her house "better than some of the services in town". Next thing the kids knew, they had done five houses in five days. With the deal Adam set up of twenty bucks for their efforts at each house, they had one hundred bucks by week's end.

"Wow, Adam!" exclaimed Tina when she saw all that money. "How much is it?" she asked with her crystal green eyes sparkling.

"One hundred big ones," Adam said. Not sure if he made it clear enough to her, "It's enough to go down to the thrift store and buy some winter clothes," Adam added.

Adam felt fairly confident that momma would see to it that they got winter coats. Even with the way she treated them, he still loved her and had secret hopes that someday she would change. Adam and Tina returned to school oblivious to the fact that their lives were in any way different than their classmates.

Adam must have been asked fifty different times about what he did over fall break. Adam was pleased to tell how he and his sister made big bucks doing odd jobs for people. He proudly announced who his customers were. Some of the boys were indifferent toward his business skills; some thought it was cool. But when Sue piped in and asked, "How much did you make, Adam?" Adam responded with the biggest smile ever,

"A hundred bucks!"

"Wow!" exclaimed Sue. "That's a lot. I like a man who knows how to work hard," she added.

You could have pushed Adam over with a feather. His face turned red and his hands began to sweat. "Uh, uh, really?" fumbled Adam.

"Yep. My mom said that the only kind of man to marry is a hardworking man," Sue replied confidently. With that the bell rang and class began.

Adam's mind was swimming with thoughts of "the good life" and marrying Sue.

"Adam. Adam. Hey Adam!" Mrs V. tried three times to peel Adam off the ceiling. She noticed the far off look in his eyes and his slight smile. She had been teaching fifth and sixth graders for twenty years now and probably could have told you his thoughts.

Adam snapped to, "Yes, yes ma'am."

Of course this got a slight laugh out of the other kids, while Sue turned and gave him a quick smile. Adam was so lost he almost forgot his name!

Money, success, marriage – all of it started to really consume Adam's thoughts. It would seem that having such a poor example of marriage would cause Adam to run from it. Why he hadn't even had a girlfriend yet. However, Adam was convinced he could do better than his own parents. Adam wasn't afraid of marriage. He wanted it. *Why* he wanted it he did not know.

Later that night, after Tina was asleep and after a brief encounter with his mother, Adam went back to his dream land. Today marked a significant day in a young boy's psyche. Adam was elated to realize that he had the skills to make big money and attract a beautiful young girl's attention. "I got noticed," Adam said in a soft low voice. "Wow, I got noticed!"

The feelings and emotions Adam experienced could have been measured with a thermometer. His commitment to study and work hard intensified. Why, you would have thought he had just finished Harvard School of Business and been hired by the largest stock firm in Chicago! Adam laid awake for hours playing the day over and over in his mind, adding to it each time. Exhaustion eventually took over and he drifted off to sleep.

Adam's confidence grew and his grades continued to improve. Adam found his identity in a job well done and school had taken on a whole new importance. Adam began to treat school as a job. He held tight to Mr. Horton's motto that "Good grades mean a good job." Adam didn't understand what it meant to be a child. Being carefree and playful were not experiences that he knew. They were replaced with adjectives such as "drive, commitment, excellence, power, control, perseverance, and self-preservation."

Adam also began to realize that Tina was his life. Other than being in different grades and at opposite ends of the school building, they were inseparable. That fact did not bother him in any way. Underneath it all, Tina was another way that Adam felt validated and needed. No matter what happened to their parents, no one could take Tina from him or him from Tina.

With that thought on his mind, Adam reassured Tina that he would always be there to take care of her. Tina smiled and said, "I know, Adam."

"Where are we going to work today?" Tina asked.

"Mrs Newsome has hired us to do a really good cleaning in her basement," answered Adam. "She is having family visit for Thanksgiving and that is only a couple of weeks away. So, finish your breakfast. It's almost 7:30."

Tina had noticed that she felt more tired lately, and a bit sluggish. She wasn't going to say anything to Adam, though. He had enough to worry about, she reasoned. Even at seven years old she had become very perceptive to what was happening to them.

Tina had become the star student of her class. Being smart, pretty, and friendly had won her many friends and the praise of her teacher, Ms. Sherry. Tina was outgoing and played with everyone. Even though Adam had said they needed to be loners at home didn't mean she had to be one at school.

Tina managed to get through the day of work but she couldn't hide the fact that she was really tired. Adam was oblivious as he hurried to finish up before dark, which he knew would approach around 5pm.

They began walking home close to 4pm. The

temperature held at about forty degrees with no clouds in the sky and no snow to wade through, which made the walk much easier.

Adam noticed that Tina wasn't walking beside him; she was quiet and seemed distracted.

"Hey, you okay, sis?"

"I don't know. I guess I'm really tired or something," replied Tina.

Adam smiled, "Sure you are. You worked really hard today! I am very proud of you. Hey, get in the wagon and I'll pull you the rest of the way home."

"Thanks Adam," Tina said as she climbed in.

Tina took her bath and got ready for bed while Adam cleaned up from dinner; then she joined him in the kitchen.

"Adam, I miss momma a lot. Will you tell her to come and tuck me in when she gets home?"

Adam could barely stand to look at his sister. Her eyes were red and sad as if she had been crying. Her cheeks seemed sunken in a little and her color was rather pale.

"Tina," Adam tried not to sound alarmed as he asked, "Are you okay?"

"I feel tired is all," Tina said softly.

"Well, tomorrow is Sunday so you should sleep in," replied Adam. "We don't have any work to do. Come on, I'll tuck you in, and I promise as soon as momma gets home I'll tell her you want to be tucked in."

"Okay, thank you, Adam," said Tina.

$$\bullet \ \bullet \ \bullet \ \bullet \ \bullet$$

Sunday was pretty typical, except that Tina slept in until eleven.

"Wow, you sure slept in late, little sis. Do you feel better?"

"Kinda, I guess," Tina said. "I was glad when momma tucked me in."

Adam was confused by Tina's statement. He knew his momma was home, but *when* she got home, he didn't know. He almost always woke up when she came through the door, though he pretended to still be asleep.

Adam continued fixing lunch for Tina, momma, and himself. It was always hit or miss if momma ate or not, but to Adam's surprise, she did.

"Momma," Adam said cautiously. "Tina isn't feeling very good. Do you think she should go to the doctor?"

"What's wrong, Tina?" momma asked.

"I just feel tired a lot, I guess. I'm not very hungry, either," Tina responded.

"Well, uhmm, just rest up today and we will see how you feel tomorrow," momma said. "In fact, why don't you go on and lie down now?"

"Okay, momma," replied Tina.

After Tina left the room, Adam asked, "Do you think she will be okay, Momma?"

"Sure, it's probably just a bug going around. A woman from work said her boy has had a bug lately. So, don't worry. Just keep an eye on her."

Adam nodded, but wasn't convinced.

"Look, Adam, I have to work tonight. Some big wigs have come to town."

"On Sunday, Momma?" Adam almost couldn't believe he questioned her.

"It doesn't matter what day it is, work is work!" she fired back. "Now look, Adam, here is fifty bucks. Go to the store and buy some food. I won't be leaving until 4 p.m. or so; that way Tina won't be alone."

"Yes ma'am," Adam answered.

As Adam cleaned up from lunch his thoughts were on a million things. "What's wrong with Tina.... Why is momma working on Sunday....Where is dad?" Adam thought back to the last time his dad was home and could barely remember one good thing about it. "Probably just as well that he isn't here," Adam said aloud to himself.

Adam glanced in to see if Tina was asleep, then put on his sweatshirt and jacket to head to the store. As he walked out the door he noticed a fancy red sports car pulled into his driveway.

"Hey kiddo, is Amber home?"

"I don't know anyone named Amber," Adam replied. Adam was amazed at the amount of make-up and perfume this lady was wearing. She was tall and shapely, with real thick blond hair that went below her shoulders. "Probably would have been prettier without the make-up," Adam thought to himself. Adam's momma didn't wear make-up like that, she was pretty enough without it.

"Oh, I'm sorry cutie, I meant Shirley. I sometimes call her Amber as a nickname, ya know."

"Yeah, sure," Adam said. "I'l...."

"Hey Trixy, get in here before you get cold!" interrupted momma.

"Gotta go kiddo. You sure are cute though," Trixy said, making her way into the house.

All the way to the store, Adam kept thinking how strange it was that someone stopped by. He had never seen that woman before, or even heard her name. "Oh well, I better stay focused on grocery shopping."

Even though it was Thanksgiving season the store was decorated for Christmas. They even played Christmas music over the P.A. system. It wasn't that Adam didn't like Christmas, it just wasn't a big deal at his house. In fact, he didn't have a single significant Christmas memory. One time he and Tina had received a few packages with sweaters in them from some aunt in Iowa that he had never met.

Adam hurried along the aisles picking out easy to fix meals. Soups, peanut butter, lunch meat, frozen tater tots, fish sticks, crinkle fries, and things like that. Adam walked by those big Butterball Turkeys and wondered about how good they would be. "No chance of me fixing one of those," Adam said and moved along.

Adam rounded the dairy aisle and came to the beer coolers, but instead of stacks of beer and football stuff there was a manger scene in their place.

Adam paused to listen to the recording. "Then an angel of the Lord stood before them, and the glory of the Lord shone around them, and they were terrified. But the angel said to them, "Don't be afraid, for look, I proclaim to you good news of great joy that will be for all the people. Today a Savior, who is Christ the Lord, was born for you in the city of David. This will be a sign for you: you will find a baby wrapped snugly in swaddling clothes and lying in a manger...Glory to God in the highest heaven, and peace on earth to people and good will to men." (Luke 2:9-12, 14)

Adam flashed back in his mind to an easier, more peaceful time, when his grandma Mag took him to Sunday School a few times. He remembered the songs they sang about a baby born in a manger, named Jesus. People sing them around Christmas time. Another one was "Jesus Loves The Little Children"...It had been so long he had forgotten the words. When grandma Mag died so did most of the good days. "No time to waste," Adam said, bringing himself back to reality. "I have to get home, Tina will need me."

Even though he had thirty minutes to spare

the tongue-lashing came. "Where have you been so long? What took so long?? You know how I hate to wait!" Adam was certain that if Trixy (if that was her real name) hadn't been there, his mother's anger would have been worse.

"Oh leave the kiddo alone. We have plenty of time Shirley," came Trixy to the rescue, from what seemed like a never ending barrage of questions, that of course he would never have a chance to answer. "Besides, now that he's back we can leave early. Ya know how the bosses hate to be kept waiting," Trixy said.

With that the two burst out laughing. "Yeah, you're right," replied Shirley. "Hey, look Adam, Tina is in her room playing. Don't stay up late, you both have school in the morning. Ya know, you're the man of the house."

"Yes ma'am."

That was the end of the discussion between Adam and momma. Shirley and Trixy walked out giggling and joking quietly about the bosses.

Adam had a bunch of questions on his mind – "Who is Trixy?...Why were they dressed like they were going to a party instead of work? And where was work anyway?" Adam remembered that some of the boys at school knew where their parents worked…but why didn't he?

"Adam, you're home!" Tina said excitedly, bringing Adam back to reality.

"Hey sis, you alright?

"Yeah, I think so. I don't feel so tired anyway."

"Good, I'm glad," Adam said with a smile. "Come into the kitchen and you can pick out what you want for supper."

During supper Tina asked Adam about Christmas. "Adam, do you think momma will buy us some presents? Or will she let Santa Claus come by, like he goes to Johnny's house? Johnny says Santa Claus brings him presents every year."

Tina sure must have gotten some energy back; the questions came quick, like a machine gun fired them.

"Well, ummm, I don't know Tina. I guess we could ask her."

"We certainly have been good, don't ya think Adam?"

Adam assured Tina that he would talk to momma soon about it.

The next few weeks went by quickly. Both Adam and Tina had some small parties, and even some plays at school. Christmas was four weeks away and only three of those would be spent at school. Winter break would last till January 3rd. Adam remembered his promise to Tina that he would talk to momma about Santa Claus.

Picking the right time to get momma's attention about such an unimportant thing wasn't going to be easy. But he had promised Tina, and no matter what, he had to follow through. It was early Saturday morning and Tina was still asleep. Adam could hear the T.V. on in his momma's room.

With a timid knock on the bedroom door Adam quietly called out, "Momma? Momma, you awake?" Adam was nervous but determined that he had to ask today. Christmas was only three weeks away.

"Yeah, you can come in. I can hardly hear you through the door," came his mother's response.

Adam stood at the end of the bed, rather surprised to see his momma so awake.

"What is it Adam?"

"Umm, I promised Tina (using that as motivation not to back out) that I would ask you if Santa Claus could come to our house this year. We have both been really good, I think."

"You think? Well, have you or not? Aren't you sure?"

"Yes ma'am, I am sure!" Adam said as he straightened up and threw his chest out.

"Well well, don't you have some attitude," his mother responded.

Adam's face went pale and his hands began to sweat.

His mother continued, "I wondered how long it would be before you got it, or if you would ever get it. I tell you, your daddy never had it. He was a weak snake. Boy, let me tell you, real women want a man that will stand up and say what he means and get what he wants."

You could have knocked Adam over with a feather. He just stood there as his mother went on about how a real man acts, not leaving out the details about how a real man treats a woman. Of course she managed to slip in several references to how poor of a man his daddy was. Nonetheless, Adam heard every word and committed them to memory. This was a very important day for him, and in a small way, he felt validated by his mother.

"Well, I suppose if I am gonna invite Santa Claus to come here you two better get on with making a list of a few things you want. And I mean a *few* things."

"You mean we can say what we want?" Adam asked.

"Why of course! How else will he know what to bring. Get the lists to me by tomorrow afternoon."

"Yes ma'am!" Adam said excitedly. "We will, for sure!"

Adam wanted to rush to Tina's room to tell her but she was still sleeping. "I'd better wait, she needs her rest anyway." So Adam sat down at the table and thought hard and long about a few things he would want. Maybe a new radio, or some puzzles. "I sure liked putting the puzzle together with Tina." How about a new shirt and pants, and a new belt. "Nah," Adam said, "I will get the clothes later."

Tina slipped in the chair next to Adam so

quietly he almost didn't notice her.

Sleepy eyed and with a big yawn, Tina said, "Good morning, Adam. Whatcha doin'?"

"Hey sis, great news! Momma said she will invite Santa Claus to come to our house. And we get to make a list of a few things we want."

"Really!? Oh boy! I know what I want!"

"You do?" Adam replied.

"Yep, I've been thinkin' about it a lot," responded Tina.

"Well okay. Here is a piece of paper for you to write it down."

Ken and Barbie dolls and cars.

"Wow, Tina. Your writing is getting so much better."

"Thank you, Adam. Adam, do you think Santa Claus will really do it…I mean bring it?"

"Yeah, sure Tina. I know he likes to see kids smile."

"Oh yeah," Tina agreed, while she searched her memory for the last time she saw him at K-Mart

• • • • •

It was the week before Christmas and Tina was so excited she talked about nothing else except how she was going to play with the Barbie doll. She was going to dress her up so Ken would take her out on a date. Adam was looking forward to his new radio and a book about Chicago. But the real question on his mind – whether Santa was real or not – was would his mother come through?

Adam was sent to the store alone while his momma was home with Tina. He decided to buy Tina a few small toys from the sale bin and some candy. For momma, a flower in a plexy glass bowl and some chocolate. He knew it had been a long time since she got a flower and candy – if ever. He bought everything with the money left over from the summer jobs. He even bought the wrapping paper for fifty cents. Adam had learned to bargain shop, but deep down he wanted to buy expensive things for Tina, and make sure that she had the best of everything. "Someday," Adam mumbled to himself. "Someday I'll make it big."

Christmas Eve was very different. Adam, Tina, and even momma sat in front of the T.V. watching Rudolph the Red Nose Reindeer and Frosty the Snowman.

"Kids, you need to be goin' to bed now. Santa Claus won't stop by if he sees you up."

Adam smiled while Tina jumped up and down shouting, "Really? Really!?" You mean you told him he could come by?"

"Yes, I sure did, little girl, and you know what he said?"

"No, what? What momma, what did he say?"

Tina said excitedly.

"He said that since you two were so well behaved he would stop here first."

"You mean it? Wow! Thanks momma." And with that Tina wrapped herself around momma, hugging and giving her kisses.

"Okay, okay. You're welcome," momma said.

With that Adam looked at momma and said, "Thank you." She smiled, tussled his hair, and shooed him off to bed. For the first time in over a year momma carried Tina to bed and tucked her in.

After she pulled her children's bedroom doors closed, momma made her way to the living room to set out a few decorations and two stockings – one for Adam and one for Tina. Both were overflowing with odds and ends. Things for girls and things for boys.

Then she proceeded to set out the big gifts. For Tina, Barbie and Ken dolls, complete with a red convertible corvette; a Barbie doll house and all the furnishings; a toy kitchen set complete with dishes and pots and pans; an assortment of coloring books and a fifty piece crayon set; two new sweaters and two pairs of blue jeans. For Adam, a new AM/FM radio with a cassette player; a twenty dollar gift certificate for K-Mart to pick out his own music; a book on the facts about Chicago by Encyclopedia Britannica, complete with color pictures and maps; a Webster's dictionary; a calculator; a journaling book; one pair of blue jeans, one pair of black corduroy pants, and a navy blue Chicago Bears sweatshirt.

Shirley sat back and took inventory. Sadly enough, if the kids hadn't told her what they wanted it would have been all guess work. She really didn't know her children at all.

Thirty-two year old Shirley Marie Windsor lit a few candles, sat down in the living room, and began to cry. The guilt, shame, anger, remorse, and bitterness of her life overwhelmed her. This wasn't the life she dreamed of as a little girl. She thought back to when Adam was born and the promises she had made to always take care of him. By the time Tina came along her life was a mess. She had become an alcoholic and her husband, who was a drug addict, had begun dealing to support his habit. The pregnancy had shocked her enough to think about aborting, but she couldn't find the nerve to go through with it.

She recalled the many, many fights that took place before her husband finally walked out. She was left alone to fend for herself and two young children. Then Trixy came along – her real name was Nancy – and turned her onto prostitution to make a few quick bucks and get by until she could get a real job. That was two years ago. She felt trapped. The alcohol numbed the pain and the men that bought her validated her.

After she cried for a while and asked "who knows who" why her life was such a mess she made her way to her bedroom and pulled out the bottle of whisky she kept hidden in a drawer. With two large drinks she went to sleep.

Early Christmas morning Shirley woke up. It was 4:30. "I'd better pull myself together," she said to herself. She promised herself that she would stop drinking and prostituting soon. Of course she put a condition on it – "as soon as I get a little more money saved up. Besides as long as the kids don't know it won't hurt them." She was oblivious to the damage she had already done to Adam and Tina.

Shirley poured herself a cup of coffee and sat on the couch. She looked over the bounty of gifts and managed to smile. She wouldn't wake them; she decided to wait to see who would emerge first. She was surprised that it was Tina.

Tina ran out dragging her pink bunny with her. When she saw all the gifts she screamed, "Momma! Momma! Look at all this stuff!"

Adam bolted out of bed and ran to the living room. He shouted for joy and danced with Tina.

"Kids! Kids! Hey, I know you're excited but keep it down or you'll wake the dead."

"Okay momma," they said in unison. Then they began to look at the name tags.

In all the excitement Adam almost forgot the gifts he bought for momma and Tina. Adam retrieved the gifts and quickly presented them. Momma cried and shook her head in disbelief.

"Son, how did you buy these?"

"Me and Tina worked odd jobs this past summer and I saved up."

Shirley was ashamed to think how she had abandoned her own children, but she managed to commend them for being so responsible.

"Kids, I am very proud of you both. Now go on, open your gifts."

The whole day was full of play. Adam even let himself play with his sister – he was Ken, of course. They had a tea party and imaginary cookies after lunch. Tina was exhausted and fell asleep on the floor. Momma had fallen asleep on the couch but Adam was too excited to read about Chicago to fall asleep. Who could have known how important a day, today, would prove to be?

Three
Broken Promises

Christmas was gone as quickly as it had come. Life for the Windsor family took on an all too familiar routine. Momma was gone just as much as before while Adam and Tina stayed busy shoveling snow. The evenings were spent playing with Tina's new toys and when she fell asleep Adam pulled out his book about Chicago.

· · · · ·

The courtroom was more intimidating than she thought it would be. Shirley Marie Windsor sat in the defendant's seat with the public defender. Of course he was also there to help defend the many others caught in the prostitution sting.

"Ms. Windsor, have you ever been in trouble with the law before?" asked the public defender. He was about 5'10", probably two hundred pounds, with dark hair parted to one side, somewhere around 40 years old.

Shirley stumbled over her words, still hung over. She spent the night on a concrete bench in the county lock-up, cold and unable to sleep. The endless chatter and curses that came from the "pros", as she called them, were still ringing in her ear.

"No sir, I haven't," she finally said.

"Okay, then maybe I can get the D.A. to agree to a warning and a small fine. The judge though, he's a mean ol' cuss, been doin' this for years. Although I have seen him give a few breaks lately; and with it bein' the holidays, who knows today might be your lucky day," the public defender reassured her.

The reality and severity of Shirley's crime became very obvious as the judge handed out seven and ten days in the county lock-up to those before her. "What about my kids?" she thought to herself. "What will happen to them?" she wondered.

"Shirley Marie Windsor, step to the podium please," came the command from the large bailiff who was standing near the judge's bench. Fixing her shirt and running her fingers through her long brown hair, Shirley stepped up to the microphone and waited.

The judge, a white-haired man with glasses that sat on the end of his nose, appeared to be reading from some papers as he mumbled and pursed his lips.

"Miss Windsor!" the judge's voice boomed through the courtroom, "You're quite a bit a ways from home."

Shirley just stared at the judge, not sure if he was expecting an answer or not. The public defender gave her a little nudge, "Yes sir. Thirty five miles I guess."

The pro's sitting in the gallery whispered and commented to each other on the fact that Shirley was doing great at playing the part of a rookie. They eagerly awaited the response to the judge's next question. They had heard it lots of times.

"Ms. Windsor, don't you know that you cannot obtain a business license in the City of Champaign for prostitution? And since you can't get a business license for prostitution, that makes it illegal."

Shirley, as calm and collected as she could be replied, "I do now, your Honor."

The crowded courtroom burst into laughter, along with the bailiff. The judge got his courtroom back in order, peered over the top of his glasses and said, "I guess you must be a rookie."

"Your Honor, what my client…."

"Hold on, counselor. I think I understand. Ms. Windsor, let me tell you as clear as I can…" The judge went on for about 10 minutes telling Shirley, and anyone else who cared to listen, what he would do if she ever stepped foot in his courtroom again.

"…And so, Ms. Windsor, I am going to let you off with a warning and a thirty dollar fine for court costs." With that the judge slammed down his gavel. "Next case," he hollered.

Trixy scurried out of the courtroom to wait for Shirley. Trixy was one of the few who didn't get "caught up" the night before.

"Girl, you did great!" came Trixy's congratulations.

"Like a real pro," she added.

"Well, I don't feel like a 'real pro'. I thought I was going to throw up."

"Hey, don't let it get you. We all have faced a judge or two in our days."

Trixy could tell that Shirley was pretty down and needed a boost. "Come on, Shirley, drinks are on me. There's a really neat lounge around the corner."

"No, I don't think so," Shirley said as she rubbed her forehead. "I need to go home."

"Go home!?" Trixy sounded stunned at the thought. "All ya need is a couple stiff drinks and bam, good as new - hair of the dog."

Shirley knew what "hair of the dog" meant – pour alcohol on your hangover and you'll bounce right back.

"Come on Shirley, just a couple of drinks and then you can go home." Trixy was really good at manipulation. She used it to get extra money out of her "tricks".

"Well, just a couple," Shirley said weakly.

"That's my girl. Who knows, we might see some good looking guys."

After they arrived at the lounge Shirley cleaned up in the ladies room while Trixy scoped out the best table to sit at. The warmth of the lounge and the low lighting felt good to Shirley, compared to the coldness and brightness of the courtroom.

• • • • •

Adam checked the clock on the wall for the tenth time – 4:30. The two of them had been home from school since 3:00. Adam was scared that something very serious had happened to momma. He hadn't seen her since early the morning before. Of course he kept all of this to himself; there was no way he could let Tina know.

Adam checked on Tina who was working on her homework. He helped her with her math, including the flash cards, then he gave her a spelling test. He made sure to repeat each word twice like Ms. Sherry.

"And use it in a sentence, Adam," was Tina's final instruction.

"I know, I know. I've had lots of spelling tests."

Adam was lying on the couch finishing his reading assignment for English when Tina joined him in the living room. She plopped down on the bean bag. She was quiet and seemed to be thinking about something serious.

"Adam, why isn't momma home? Why does she stay gone so much? Doesn't she love us anymore?" Tina just stared at him waiting for a response.

Adam was faced with the questions that he hoped he would never have to answer. He closed his eyes and began to search for all the right words to comfort his sister. Of course these were the very same questions he had asked himself many times before. Adam decided to answer Tina the very same way he answered himself, "I don't know," he said as he dropped his gaze to the floor.

Several minutes passed before Adam looked up and made an effort to comfort his sister – maybe he was really trying to convince himself. Tina seemed okay with his usual answers.

"I'm sure she loves us. And I'm pretty sure she is alright. Also, I will tell her when she gets home to come and tuck you in, Okay?"

"Okay," Tina replied.

"Sis, are you sure all your homework is done?"

"Yep, I'm sure."

Well, do you want me to tuck you in?" Adam offered.

"Yes, please."

• • • • •

Momma walked through the door at 11:30pm. Adam pretended to be a sleep as he heard his momma stagger across the living room toward her bedroom. The last thing he needed was to talk to her while she was drunk. He was content that she came home and came home alone. Adam was thankful that Tina didn't have to see her momma like that.

The next morning Adam went through his usual routine. He checked to see if his momma was awake, but today was different. Adam began to feel a strong hate for his mother. He didn't even try to wake her up; he just stared down at her, "What's the use? I guess you really don't care, and he left the room.

• • • • •

The only thing that changed about Shirley was her routine. She and Trixy decided to work a different hotel for a few weeks. Trixy had convinced Shirley that the vice squad just needed their pound of flesh and what better time to get it than the holidays.

"Makes great news," Trixy said. "I guess it makes the mayor look good, ya know, tough on crime," she added.

As time went by Adam didn't even notice or care if his mother was home or not. The notes and money on the counter were enough for him. His only concern was taking care of Tina and keeping her busy. Even the lies he told her, about where momma was, had become easy. Adam simply reasoned, "She's too young; it would hurt her too much."

Winter seemed to hang on forever in the prairie land of Illinois. Adam and Tina spent the last weekend of February shoveling snow. Adam agreed with Tina that it was much easier to mow grass than shovel snow.

"This is the wet heavy stuff. I'm sure looking forward to the summer and the green grass," Adam said.

"Yeah, me too, Adam. My lungs are burning."

"What do you mean sis?"

"It's like it's hard to breathe, or maybe they are just cold. Like when I put my cold hands under warm water and they hurt." Tina did the best she could to describe how she felt.

"Hey, we are almost finished. Why don't you go and ask if you can warm up inside and I'll finish up the sidewalk."

About 15 minutes later Adam rang the doorbell. Mrs. Wilson answered, "Come in, Adam, and warm up a bit before you head home."

Tina smiled big when Adam entered the kitchen. "Mrs. Wilson is so nice. Look, she gave me hot chocolate and cookies!"

"Here Adam," Mrs. Wilson said, setting a mug of hot steamy chocolate with whip cream on the table. "Do you want some cookies?"

"Yes ma'am. That would be great."

The children really enjoyed working for Mrs. Wilson. She was one of their regular customers. They mowed, raked, weeded, cleaned, and even washed her car a time or two. Mrs. Wilson was a retired school teacher and had traveled around the world with her husband who was an Air Force Pilot. She would entertain the children with many stories of the places she had been and all the children she had taught.

"Oh my! You two better get going home. It will be dark soon."

"Yes ma'am," and off they went.

• • • • •

"Tina, are you alright?" Adam couldn't hide the

alarm in his voice.

"I don't think so," Tina said sluggishly. "I feel really cold and shaky."

"Let me feel your forehead. Whoa! It's crazy hot, Tina."

"But I feel cold."

"Okay, uhmm, let's get you wrapped up in something warm. Can you go change into your pj's? You can't wrap up with wet pants on."

When Tina returned Adam was frantic. He didn't have a clue how to fight a fever. "Here Tina, I think these baby aspirins will help. I'll look to see if we have a thermometer. Here, lie down on the couch and cover up."

After searching through the bathroom cabinets and finally finding a thermometer he returned to Tina. "Tina, open up. I washed it. I don't know much about how these things work so I'll just check here in a few minutes."

"Mmmhmm," Tina mumbled in agreement.

Adam just stared at her; she couldn't even keep her eyes open. Adam was scared and wasn't sure if he should run to the neighbors house or not - their home phone hadn't worked in weeks – but he couldn't leave Tina alone.

"Maybe momma will be home soon," Adam said as he re-tucked the blanket around her.

The thermometer read 102, he was sure of that, and Tina's head was on fire. "I will get you a cold rag for your head," Adam said, but never mentioned the temperature.

"Where is momma?"

"What am I supposed to do now?!" Adam thought to himself. He was in a fit and yet did everything he could to keep Tina calm and tucked in.

Tina moaned and squirmed on and off; Adam kept applying cold rags and giving her water to drink. Several hours later the fever broke. Tina was drenched in sweat and her hair was matted down with it. Leaving Tina on the couch covered up, Adam fought to stay awake until his momma got home. Unfortunately fatigue took over and he fell sound asleep on the floor next to the couch.

When Adam woke the next morning on the floor, he found Tina sound asleep on the couch where he had left her. Placing his hand on her forehead he was relieved to find it normal - he felt his just to be sure.

Now to decide what to do about school...Adam knocked rather hard on his momma's bedroom door.

"Momma, are you awake?" With no response Adam repeated his question a little louder.

"Ya, huh, who is it?"

"Momma, it's Adam. I need to talk to you. It's important. Tina's sick!"

"Hold on, hold on. Just give me a minute."

Adam stood outside the door with a mixture of fear for Tina and anger at momma.

"Okay, you can come in. Now, what did you say about Tina and a stick?"

"No momma, Tina is sick. Last night she had a fever. The thermometer said 102 degrees. What are we supposed to do?"

As momma got up she said she would check on her.

"Tina, honey?" momma gently nudged her awake.

"Momma!" Tina said in a groggy, weak voice.

"Hey baby, how do you feel?"

"Better I guess. I don't feel cold or anything."

"Okay good. I'm going to take your temperature, okay?"

"Okay momma."

Shaking the thermometer down momma placed it under Tina's tongue. "Adam, why don't you get Tina and me some water?"

"Yes ma'am. Is she going to be okay?"

"Sure, probably just a bug or something."

Adam returned with two glasses of water. "Well, your temperature is up a little, 100 degrees. That's not too bad," said momma, trying to comfort Tina and Adam.

"Adam, you go on and go to school and I will take care of Tina."

Adam was not sure how to take what he had just heard. Go to school and leave Tina? Momma is going to take care of Tina??

"I promised Tina I would take care of her,"

Adam said out loud.

"Adam! I said go to school! I will take care of Tina!"

Adam, it's okay. I'll be fine," said Tina, doing her level best to encourage Adam not to argue with momma.

Adam got changed for school, grabbed his backpack, and made one last check on Tina before heading out.

Adam was worried sick all morning; he was very distracted and inattentive. During the first break Mrs. V. asked Adam what was going on with him.

"Mrs. V., Tina is really sick at home and I'm worried about her."

"Oh, I see. Is your mother with her?"

"Yes ma'am." Adam was less than confident in his response.

"Well I'm sure your mother knows what she is doing. We mothers have a built in skill for taking care of our babies."

Adam wanted to say, "Momma is horrible at taking care of her babies!" but thought he better keep that to himself.

Mrs. V. could see Adam's far off look and knew she wasn't making any headway. "Well Adam, I tell you what. If you try not to worry so much I will switch this afternoon up and we will all have a fun day, okay?"

"I'll try," Adam agreed.

During that recess Mrs. V tried to call the Windsor home to check on Tina and hopefully give Adam some good news. To her surprise the phone operator recording said, "The number you have dialed has been disconnected. If you…" click. Mrs. V. knew the rest of the recording. Checking the number again she dialed and got the same result. Mrs. V. reasoned that there was no reason to call the employer listed since Adam said his mother was home with Tina. Replacing the information card back in his records file she returned to the classroom.

• • • • •

"The doctor will see you now. Hey sweetie, not feeling so well, huh?" the nurse said as she led them into an exam room at the free clinic. The only thing separating one exam room from another were the white curtains that could be opened by sliding them one way or the other on silver rods. Aside from a few babies crying in the background the clinic was surprisingly quiet and well organized.

Another nurse came in and recorded necessary information. Name, birthdate, symptoms, etc.

"Here honey, can you sit up here on this table?" The nurse was polite and gentle with Tina, and genuinely seemed to care about her. "You know what?" the nurse asked Tina excitedly.

Tina was about to ask "what?" when the nurse went to….

"I have a niece whose name is name is Tina also, and she is 11 years old."

"My brother is 11, and his name is Adam." Tina seemed to struggle with her words and was beginning to shiver.

"Oh sweetie, I'm sorry. No more questions. Let me get your temperature."

101 degrees, was the reading.

About then the doctor entered the room. "Hi there, honey." She was about 30, tall with long red hair and pretty eyes. Tina liked her right away because of her smile and how nice she was. "Well, let's see what's going on with you."

The doctor checked Tina's eyes, throat, ears, listened to her heart and her lungs. And during all of that she asked mom a bunch of questions. "Has anyone else in the home been sick? How about allergies?...Foods?...Animals? Have you been out of the country? How long has this fever been going on?"

Shirley did her best to keep up with the doctor, at least enough to satisfy her major questions. "Well doctor, what's wrong with her?" momma finally got one of her own questions in.

"Well, her lungs have some fluid buildup which indicates pneumonia. And her blood pressure is a little low. I am going to prescribe an antibiotic for the pneumonia. Also, give her children's Bayer aspirin, and lots of liquid, like juice, and water." Turning to Tina, the doctor went on, "Bed rest, young lady. I mean no running around, okay honey?"

"Yes ma'am."

After giving the nurse some more instructions the doctor stroked Tina's hair down and left.

· · · · ·

Adam did his best not to worry about Tina, and Mrs. V. did her best to keep a lively and entertaining class going. Mrs. V. knew full well that Adam was committed to taking care of Tina – she just didn't know the depth of that commitment or the real reason behind it.

At 2:25 it seemed as though Adam was posed in a runner's stance waiting for the gun to fire. 2:30 just couldn't get there quick enough for him. The bell rang and Adam was off! Adam sprinted the whole mile and a half home.

Crashing through the door out of breath Adam went looking for Tina. "There you are, Tina. Hey sis, how do you feel?"

"I don't feel so good." Tina was weak and could hardly keep her eyes open. "Adam, would you close the curtains? The sun is too bright."

"Yeah…Is that better?"

"Mmhmm."

"Do you need anything?" Adam asked her.

"I'm thirsty."

"Okay, what do you want?"

"Momma got me some grape juice. Can I have

some more of that?"

"Sure thing, sis. I'll be right back."

Adam helped Tina sit up and fluffed her pillow for her. Then he went to find momma. Adam knocked on her bedroom door.

"Momma, are you awake?"

"Yes, Adam, you can come in."

Adam was dumbfounded to see his momma dressed in a short skirt, tight blouse, and spraying hair spray in her hair as she styled it. "Momma,you going somewhere?"

"Well, yes," momma said in a tone that suggested the obvious. "Now look Adam, I have to take care of something. I will be back after a while."

"But momma,what about Tina? What if she gets sicker?"

"Look, you can handle it. The doctor gave her some medicine. It's on the counter. Give her some more at 6pm. One tablet and some of that liquid stuff. The measure is with it. It isn't hard, Adam."

"When will you be back?"

"Look here young man, I don't answer to you!"

"But…"

"But nothing! Do as you are told!"

With that momma stopped by the couch to give Tina a kiss on the forehead and then walked out of the house.

The anger Adam felt toward his mother was beyond words. He ran to his bedroom, beat his fists into his pillow and screamed, "I hate you! I hate you! I hate you!!" The flood of tears drenched his face and mixed with his sweat. He felt tension through his whole body and began to shake and sob uncontrollably. The words coming from Adam were unintelligible and were nothing more than soft mumbles as he hugged his pillow and rocked back and forth on the edge of his bed.

Adam woke with a start, "Oh my gosh, Tina!" He found Tina asleep on the couch. "Well, it's only 5:30 so I guess I will leave her to sleep till 6:00 and then give her the medicine."

Adam needed a distraction from worry and fear. Taking his book on Chicago he settled down into the beanbag across from Tina. Adam enjoyed getting lost in the history of this famous city. He slowly began to allow his mind to wander and wonder what it would be like to live there. He discovered in his reading that there were apartments in those high rise buildings and that's where he wanted to live.

"Hey Tina. Hey sis, you need to wake up."

With a big stretch and yawn Tina told Adam she missed him.

"I missed you too. I have to give you some more medicine."

"Okay. That nice doctor lady said that it would make me better soon. Is momma home?"

"Not yet, but I'm sure she'll be here soon." Adam tried to stay upbeat and positive. And since he was feeling better – mostly because he was back in control – that wasn't too hard to do. Besides, he had begun to care less whether she was home or not.

"Tina, I'll take good care of you. I promise."

"I believe you, Adam."

Tina requested chicken noodle soup with crackers for supper. The two ate and talked about school, friends, games, and the future.

"Adam, will you tell me some more about Chic… Chica…"

"Chicago?"

"Yeah, that's it…Chicago."

Adam could talk for hours about the "Windy City." He got his book out and showed her pictures of the skyscrapers, Soldiers Field, Wriggley Stadium, The 'L' Train, Lake Michigan, and even the Chicago Mercantile Exchange.

"Wow, Adam, that lake is like the ocean. Ms. Sherry showed us pictures of the ocean and you can't see the other side."

"Yep, she's huge alright, except the ocean is salt water and Lake Michigan is fresh water – and it stays cold most of the time." Adam was relieved to see Tina was feeling well enough to stay awake.

Momma walked in the house at 9:30 pm. Adam and Tina were listening to the radio Adam had gotten for Christmas. Adam had just introduced Tina to the Chicago radio station and both were enjoying the music.

"Well, I see you must be feeling better," momma said as she sat on the couch with Tina.

"Kinda, I guess. My stomach feels like it's going in circles," Tina said as she made a circular motion on her stomach.

Adam could smell the cigarette and booze from across the room and noticed that his mother's words were a little slurred. "Oh great, this is all we need. Why didn't she just stay gone!" Adam thought to himself.

"Well I'm gonna go take a bath. Adam, keep an eye on your sister and don't keep her up late."

"Yes ma'am," Adam said through gritted teeth.

"Adam, will you turn the radio back on?" Tina asked. "It helps me not to think about my stomach."

About 30 minutes later…"Adam! I feel…" and Tina vomited.

"Oh no! Tina! Hey, you alright?" Adam wasn't sure what to ask or what to do.

"I think I'm through now," Tina said.

Adam beat on the bathroom door loud enough to be heard over the radio that his momma was listening to.

"Who is it? What do you want?"

"Momma, Tina threw up!"

"Hold on a minute!"

Momma turned the radio down, put on her robe and opened the door, "What did you say?"

"Tina threw up!"

"Well why did you let her throw up for?"

"Momma, I didn't let her. She just did it, and it's all over the blanket."

"Adam, clean up the blanket and throw it in the washer. Come here Tina. I'll wash you up in the bathroom."

Adam was scared and angry at the same time. How could his momma blame him for Tina being sick? "Did I make her sick when she got wet and cold at Mrs. Wilson's house? Is it because of all the work I had her do with me? Maybe it was that I didn't feed her good enough food?" Adam was overcome with grief and began to cry.

"Hey, why are you crying?" Momma seemed a little angry.

"I'm sorry momma if I made Tina sick. I didn't mean to."

"Well, anyway, don't cry. The doctor didn't say why she got sick. Tina is asleep in her bed now, and I'm going to bed myself." With that she turned and walked away.

Adam checked in on Tina and then went to bed in his own room across the hall from Tina. He wanted to be close in case she needed him.

"Adam. Adam," Tina said in a voice barely loud enough for him to hear.

Adam bolted from bed and ran to Tina's side, "Here I am Tina."

Tina's face was pale white and she could barely

talk. "Adam…please hug me."

Adam bent over, wrapped his arms around Tina, and placed his cheek against hers. Within seconds Tina's body went limp, her eyes closed, and she stopped breathing.

"Tina, Tina!" Adam shook Tina and yelled her name, "Tina!! Wake up Tina!!"

Adam ran to his momma's room and threw the door open as he ran through, slamming it against the wall. "Momma!" Adam shouted as he shook her.

Shirley woke up the moment Adam threw open the door but Adam was at her side before she could react.

"Adam, what? I'm awake. What's wrong?"

"It's Tina! Come on, she isn't breathing!"

Momma and Adam ran to Tina's side.

"Adam, run to the neighbors house and tell them to call an ambulance."

"Momma…"

"Now, Adam! Run!"

Adam ran as fast as he could that whole half of a mile. He screamed "Help!" as he beat furiously against the door.

Mr. Andrews answered the door quickly. "What's wrong son?"

"My…," Adam gasped for air, "My sister…We… we need an ambulance. She stopped breathing. We… we live next door that way," as Adam pointed over his left shoulder.

"Mary, call an ambulance for the Windsor house. I'm going over there."

Mr. Andrews drove Adam back in a flash and ran into the house. Momma was trying to breathe into Tina's mouth to give her some air.

"Here, let me help," Mr. Andrews said.

Adam stood in the doorway, frozen in shock and disbelief as he watched Mr. Andrews do CPR on his sister.

When the ambulance arrived Mr. Andrews told the paramedics that he had been doing CPR for 5 minutes already. They quickly loaded Tina in the ambulance and allowed momma to ride with them. Mr. Andrews agreed to bring Adam in his car and meet them at the ER.

Momma, Adam, and Mr. and Mrs. Andrews sat in a quiet room where they had been instructed to wait for the doctor.

"Shirley Windsor?"

"I'm Shirley Windsor," momma answered as she stood up.

"Please have a seat. I'm Doctor Murray. I'm sorry, we did all we could, but we just couldn't save your little girl. I am truly sorry." And with that he left the room.

Mr. and Mrs Andrews offered to help in any way they could and Mrs. Andrews began to cry. Momma dropped her head and stared at the floor in total disbelief of what she'd just heard. Adam went into shock. His mind shut down to disengage from the overwhelming grief. He couldn't even utter a word let alone cry. His whole world was gone and he felt helpless. In some way he felt that Tina's death was his fault.

After an autopsy, which was ordered by the county medical examiner due to the young age and uncertainty of death, the body was released for burial.

On the day of Tina's funeral Adam was allowed to go up to the casket alone. Tina was wearing her favorite yellow dress. She seemed like she was sleeping really soundly, and at peace in some strange way. Adam reached into his pocket to pull out the yellow hair ribbon he had given her on her 7th birthday. He placed it in Tina's hand. Then he turned around, walked over to momma, and said, "I'm ready to leave now."

"Adam, I can't leave…"

"Ms. Windsor, I'll take Adam to our house," Mr. Andrews volunteered.

"I'll stay with you, Shirley," Mary said. "Maybe it's for the best right now that Adam be able to leave. He isn't doing very well, you know."

"Well…okay then," Shirley agreed.

That was the last thing Adam remembered for the next year and a half.

Four
The Fall Out

Shirley was surprised by the number of people that visited Tina's funeral. There were people she never met, or even heard of before. Even more surprising were the number of tremendous compliments that people shared about the work that Adam and Tina did. All Shirley could do was smile and say thank you. She had no idea the impact her children made on the community.

Mrs. V. noticed some strange behaviors by Shirley Windsor that day. She nearly dismissed them, attributing them to the grief and loss she must be feeling but Mrs. V. couldn't understand how a mother could not know about her babies daily lives. Not to mention the fact that Shirley avoided every school activity.

Mrs. V. couldn't let it rest. "Something is wrong at the Windsor house," she thought. She decided to call a friend at the Department of Children and Family Services (DCFS).

After a long discussion with Ms. Andrea Miller, one of the department's top-notch investigators, she felt a little bit of relief knowing that Andrea would do a thorough investigation of the home – and especially of Shirley Windsor.

• • • • •

On a Monday morning late in March, with the approval of the DCFS director Mr. Thompson, Andrea opened a full blown investigation on Shirley Marie Windsor, the biological mother and sole caregiver of Tina Marie Windsor (deceased) and Adam Mitchell Windsor, age 11.

During her preliminary investigation, urged on by Mrs. V., Andrea discovered some disturbing facts. One was that Adam had not been attending school. Not too alarming, though, considering it had only been a few weeks since Tina's death. The real shock came when she visited the house where Adam and his mother lived.

Andrea made several attempts to contact Shirley but to no avail. The work numbers listed were no good and the house number was disconnected. After visiting with Mr. and Mrs. Andrews she decided to visit the home.

Andrea knocked on the door several times but no one answered. Then she did what all good investigators do – she started looking through windows and listening for any noises. Andrea checked the mailbox to see if there was any accumulation of old mail or newspapers. There was none.

"Something just doesn't feel right," Andrea said to herself. She decided to do a back door approach.

She drove down the road and parked her car out of site from the house. Then changed her pumps for tennis shoes and snuck back to the house, listening quietly around the windows for any sign that someone was home. She could hear Adam crying.

"Adam! Adam honey, my name is Andrea. I am a friend of Mrs. V. We are worried about you. Can you come open the door for me?"

Adam's crying became wails of horrible intensity – screams she couldn't understand.

"Adam! Adam, I am here to help you!" her voice full of fear and anxiety.

"I can't get up!" she heard amidst the sobs.

"Oh God! Lord Jesus help me to get to this child!"

Both the front and back doors had deadbolts and she couldn't get in. "Adam, hang on honey, I can't get in. I will go get help!"

Andrea phoned the police from the Andrews home. Within minutes four squad cars arrived with an ambulance and fire truck.

Within seconds the front door was knocked in by the fire department. The four police officers, followed by Andrea, rushed into the house. There she saw the worst case of abuse and neglect of her entire career.

Adam was tied up, each hand and foot tied to a corner of his bed. The bruises on his face, arms, and legs were deep black and blue. Adam was gaunt and pale. He was only wearing his underwear and a t-shirt. Adam had also urinated and defecated on himself. He was crying and screaming uncontrollably. One of the police officers yelled to get the paramedics in there.

"Be gentle with him. Please be gentle!" Andrea was doing everything she could to remain calm. "Adam, I'm Andrea. We aren't going to hurt you. We are here to help you. Can you understand what I'm saying?"

As Andrea softened her voice and continued to look into Adam's eyes his screams and wails became sniffles and gasps for air.

"Adam, these men are here to help you also. They are going to untie you now and then we are going to the hospital, okay?"

Adam's eyes fixed on Andrea's and with a slight nod of his head the ropes were cut. Adam's arms collapsed under their own weight.

"Gently, oh, be gentle," Andrea instructed them.

The paramedics gently put Adam on the stretcher and covered him up. Adam screamed and started to cry as one of the paramedics started to put the straps around Adam's legs. Andrea jumped in.

"Please don't put those straps on him. Look what he has gone through!"

"Okay, I'm sorry. I'm sorry, Adam. I didn't mean to scare you. I wasn't thinkin'."

Andrea didn't leave any chance for them to tell

her no when she stated she was riding in the ambulance with Adam.

As the ambulance was leaving the Windsor home the crime scene unit arrived, followed by two detectives who specialized in crimes against children.

The crime scene unit began to take pictures and gather physical evidence from the scene. They took the bed, mattress, and all. The two detectives questioned the officers as to what they saw and heard. Mr. and Mrs. Andrews also volunteered to give any information that might be helpful. Then the detectives left to catch up with Andrea at the hospital.

Andrea was allowed to attend the examination that Dr. Johanson performed on Adam. As the doctor recorded all the physical signs he saw on Adam's body Andrea became sick to her stomach. Deep bruising about the face, arms, upper torso, abdomen, thighs, back, buttocks, and lower legs, and rope burns on both wrists and ankles. Malnourished and pale, Adam also had high blood pressure and a fever. Dr. Johanson made it very clear, in his professional opinion, that Adam wouldn't have lived much longer under the conditions he was suffering. The doctor prescribed antibiotics, I.V. drips, x-rays, pain medicine and a mild sedative. Then he instructed the detectives and Ms. Miller that they could only stay a few minutes as Adam needed his rest.

"Adam, these men are detectives – you know what a detective is, right?" Andrea remained calm and kept her voice low. She certainly didn't want to cause Adam any more stress than he was already under.

Adam slightly nodded. Andrea smiled and said, "Okay, good."

"Adam, these men need to ask you a question, okay honey? It's very important that you be honest. And I promise, nothing will happen to you. You haven't done anything wrong."

Andrea paused and waited for Adam to agree, all the while saying a prayer under her breath that the Lord would give him strength.

"Okay," Adam said in a low whisper.

"Adam, my name is Joe. Can you tell us who did this to you?" Joe, his partner Bill, and Andrea all waited for the response.

Adam looked away towards the wall as tears started to well up in his eyes and spill down his cheeks. "Momma," he replied.

Andrea looked at Joe and then Bill in a silent confirmation of their first suspect.

Bill told them he would call the D.A., and then he left the room.

Joe gently touched Adam's hand and said, "I'm very proud of you, son. You are extremely brave."

As Joe left the room Andrea pulled up the plastic chair and sat down. She took Adam's hand and told him, "Adam, I am also very proud of you. You are quite a young man. My boss and I are going to help you in every way possible."

Adam gently closed his eyes and fell asleep. Andrea sat there a few more minutes to gather her thoughts. When the nurse came in she informed Andrea that Adam would be asleep for a while as the doctor had prescribed a pretty strong sedative.

"He needs his sleep," the nurse told her.

"I can't even imagine all the things this child will need," Andrea said as she walked out of the room.

Joe and his partner Bill were met at the hospital by the District Attorney, Brian Smith.

"Counselor, it's a little unusual to see you out to authorize a charge," Joe said.

"This sounds really bad" Brian replied, "and very technical. We all want to believe the little guy but if we don't cross our "t's" and dot our "i's" something could go wrong."

"That's what I like about you counselor," Joe replied, trying to add some humor to lighten the mood, "You're always looking out for those "i's" and "t's".

Brian and Joe went way back. They had been through some pretty ugly stuff together - although Joe couldn't recall anything this serious in his 21 years as a cop.

When Andrea joined the trio they were discussing the charges and the next move to make.

"Hello Andrea," came Brian's greeting.

"Hi Brian."

"Andrea, how is the little guy?" asked Joe.

"He's asleep. In time is outsides will heal, but what I'm worried about are his insides, his mind. Trauma is bad enough, but when it comes from the hands of a parent it will rip you apart. He will need lots of help."

"Andrea, what about his testimony?"

"Brian!" Andrea was curt but professional, "That boy has been through the worst living nightmare any horror writer could possibly think of, and you want to know about his testimony?"

"Okay, okay. I hear ya."

Andrea knew Brian well and as far as prosecutors, he was the best.

"With this list of charges she will probably cave and spill her guts to avoid a trial," said Joe.

"Well," replied Brian, "that's your job, Joe."

"Speaking of 'her'…do we know where Shirley Windsor is?" asked Andrea.

"No not yet," Bill responded. We were able to gather enough information from the house to put out an APB. Records is running her name through the system as we speak to see if she has any prior arrests."

"Rookies always eager," Joe said as he shook his head.

"Well, this a good one to get broke in on," Brian replied. The men chuckled and Andrea looked on in disgust.

"I really can't get your sick sense of humor," said

Andrea, glaring holes through all three of them.

"Sorry ma'am. I'll try to be more sensitive," said Bill.

At that moment the announcement came that Joe had a phone call. "You can take it over here in the doctor's lounge," the nurse told him.

"Well, it seems our Ms. Windsor has been busy," Joe said as he returned to the group. "Two arrests for prostitution in two different counties. We have an unmarked unit down the road from the house waiting, and a teletype has gone out to these two counties to see if their vice squads know her whereabouts." Joe's report was encouraging.

Bill responded, "Well, that will make the hay pile a little smaller."

"Goes to show you that you can take the boy out of the country but you can't take the country out of the boy," Brian chimed in.

Andrea, with a huff in her voice, said, "I have calls to make. Please keep me informed, will ya?" And off she went.

Andrea's first call was to Mr. Thompson. After explaining Adam's condition, Mr. Thompson agreed that Adam was going to need special care and psychiatric help. Mr. Thompson said that he would use his full authority with family court to get the best care for Adam that he possibly could.

"Andrea, I don't want you to get your hopes up – you know the system. Foster care is not a perfect fit for everyone."

"Yes sir, I understand. But we have to try," Andrea insisted.

Shirley Marie Windsor was taken into custody without incident, at 9:30pm on Monday March 22nd, after she entered her home. The laundry list of charges began with especially aggravated kidnapping. A class "A" felony with a maximum sentence of 25 years.

As promised Joe phoned Andrea to let her know of the arrest.

"What about bond?" Andrea was concerned that Shirley would flee.

"Brian got the judge to deny bond due to the severity of the crime. Of course, that doesn't mean that at the preliminary hearing a bond won't be set."

"I know Joe, but at least we know that Adam is safe now. Thank you for calling. Good night."

"Good night."

Andrea fell to her knees right there in her living room. "Oh God, please hear my prayer! Adam needs you. He's just a little boy! You know all that he had suffered. Please, dear Lord, heal him. In Jesus' name, amen."

Andrea began to weep over the events of the day and prayed for peace in her spirit.

Five

Black Out

No matter what clinical term you want to use for it, Adam Windsor had simply blacked out due to the physical, emotional, and psychological trauma that had been inflicted on him. Adam had become catatonic. Some days he just sat for hours staring at a wall. Some days he couldn't feed himself. Very rarely did he say anything – and when he did, it was "Tina."

Andrea and DCFS did everything they could to get Adam into the proper care facility. After several battles in front of the judge it was agreed that Adam would be placed in the State Mental Hospital, in a specialty unit designed for intensive counseling sessions. Andrea was concerned – and rightfully so – that Adam would be placed in general care and kept sedated.

Andrea petitioned the court and the director of mental health at the hospital that she be allowed to visit him since he had no family. That was easily agreed upon.

Andrea visited regularly – every Saturday morning, and when time allowed she would visit on Tuesday's as well. Adam responded very little. Andrea wasn't sure if he understood anything she talked about but she prayed daily for his recovery. And she asked for patience for herself, that she wouldn't give up.

Andrea knew all too well what it was like to be different from the other kids. Growing up she was fat, wore glasses, and kept to herself. She had her own emotional scars. It wasn't until her sophomore year of college that she realized her need of counseling.

Andrea was no stranger to church. Her mom was in the ladies guild and her dad was a deacon. She referred to her church upbringing as very staunch and rigid – she didn't know you could have a personal relationship with Jesus.

She had sought out a Christian counselor while there in college. Of course her daddy was against any outside help, but he didn't know what she was going through.

The counselor listened intently to Andrea over a period of six months. Andrea started to realize that her identity was wrapped up in what other people thought about her. The counselor began to gently introduce the truth that Jesus loved her just the way she was.

"In fact, Andrea, do you know who God the Father sees when He looks at you?"

"Well…I'm not sure," Andrea replied. "Who?"

"He sees Jesus and His righteousness, and *you* as the beautiful young lady He created for His very own purpose."

"Purpose?! What kind of purpose could God

have for a nobody like me?"

"Your sole purpose is to be the house of God. The skin that God Himself wears around. The glove that He slams His hand into. As Jesus was the incarnate God – the visible image of the Father – so we are now the visible image of Jesus to the world He has placed us into."

"What are you trying to say?"

"Andrea, it isn't what I am trying to say at all – it's what Jesus is saying to you. See Andrea, Jesus wants to be intimately involved in everything you do. Many of us grow up in church, we pray a few minutes in the morning, a few minutes at night before bed, even over meals. Of course we read the Bible here and there, but few ever pursue God. We think of God as our "co-pilot" – He's there when we really need Him, but other than that we're on our own. As a result we miss out on *knowing* Him. He wants to reveal Himself to us but He can't if we're not paying attention."

"The apostle Paul put it so well when he wrote to the church in Galatia, "But as for me, I will never boast about anything except the cross of our Lord Jesus Christ, through whom the world has been crucified to me, and I to the world" (Gal. 6:14)."

The counselor went on to explain, "What Paul said is that his focus was on Jesus. He didn't care about the world's way of doing things, or how the world viewed him. The world was dead in its control

over his mind and emotions, and since he was dead
to the world he was unable to follow its ways."

"So what you are telling me is that Jesus wants
to have a real and personal relationship with me?"

"That's it exactly – personal, up close, intimate,
even moment to moment!"

"Wow!" exclaimed Andrea, "I never knew that!
Why, then it's okay to be me, just as I am. God loves
me for me!"

Suddenly everything was different for Andrea.
She was on a whole new mission. After seeking the
Lord for direction she changed her major from business law to social work. Her new goal was to be Jesus
to whoever she came in contact with.

The battle that Adam was going through was
very dark, but she was going to be there for him, in
God's strength.

• • • • •

The legal battle was just as dark. Shirley refused
to take responsibility. She made statements such as,
"Let me talk to the boy; he will tell you the truth."

Brian had already dug in his heels and got the
judge to put a restraining order on Shirley Windsor.
There was no way she was going to get to Adam.

Delays are not uncommon in the legal system.
The first three months were wasted in preliminary
hearings and evidentiary hearings. Then Shirley fired
her public defender, which bought the D.A. another

three months. The D.A. was content to hold out for Adam's testimony, while the public defender complained about "due process".

The big question on the D.A.'s mind was whether or not Adam was mentally capable of testifying. Brian didn't want any last minute glitches if they needed to go to trial quickly.

"Let's get it all out in the open now," Brian said.

Two different psychological assessments were ordered for Shirley and the findings were the same. "Mentally stable." Brian wasn't sure if that made him feel better or not. "What kind of person – let alone a *mother*, would do this to her own child?"

Brian decided to meet with Andrea to get an update on Adam. He valued the clinical prognosis but there was something about a real personal connection that he knew would ease his mind. Besides, he couldn't postpone the trial forever – at best maybe another year or so. Fortunately there was a ton of physical evidence. The potential problem was with Adam's statement since it was retrieved under such duress. Any public defender worth his weight would turn that into "He was asking for his mother not incriminating her." And Shirley could lie and say that she left Adam in the care of "so-and-so" ... who of course would never be found. So at best she would be accused of poor judgment and a real stretch on "child endangerment". Of course Brian was in no hurry to offer a deal either.

Andrea and Brian met for coffee to discuss the case.

"Andrea, how is Adam?" Brian asked.

"Physically he has healed, but emotionally I see almost no progress."

"Is he saying much?"

"No," Andrea responded, "Not so much in words. At times his eyes will light up like a happy thought went through his mind, and at other times a tear will form. I get the feeling that he won't let himself cry. In fact I have spoken to several people who knew Adam and Tina and most of them were shocked that Adam didn't cry at the funeral. Dr. Gibbs claims that the blackout started the morning Tina died. The interesting thing about that is that Adam may remember many things, even tragic things, such as the death of his sister, looking in the casket, even telling his mother that he was ready to leave the funeral, but nothing else until he comes out of this mental shutdown."

"You mean he may not remember the beatings and being tied up?"

"That's very possible," Andrea answered, "Prior beatings and such, maybe he will – if in fact they happened."

"Come on Andrea, if? Maybe? You've worked in this field long enough."

"I know what you're after Brian but if by chance it isn't there you can't force it on him. He will most likely shut down again and that would be tragic!"

"Yeah, you're right. I don't want to do that."

"The best we can do, Brian, is to wait and pray. I know one thing for certain – that God's timing is perfect. I am confident that His hand is in this mess somehow."

"Okay Andrea. I'm willing to wait…and pray." Andrea knew Brian's faith was a little shaky but when it came right down to it his heart was in the right place.

"Well Andrea…what do you think about me visiting Adam?... with you there of course."

"Well of course - he is your client after all. I will be there on Saturday."

• • • • •

Andrea asked Brian to wait outside in the sunroom area while she went to get Adam. Andrea stopped to talk with a few of the caregivers on duty that morning to check on Adam's progress over the past week. To her delight Adam seemed to be more interactive and may have made a friend with a boy named Billy.

Billy was a few years older than Adam but he suffered from a very similar black out. The staff seemed excited about Adam's progress, which encouraged Andrea. Of course, it was too early to tell what this would mean.

The staff paid very close attention to Adam for

any regression chronologically. There was the possibility that Adam could regress to an earlier age in order to break through the black out and the catatonic state he was in. The goal of the treatment plan was to keep him at the age he is developing at as he gets older. This was such a critical age, so much going on in a young boy's mind, not to mention his growing body and changing needs. Adam's motor skills were good and he appeared to be growing and changing like most 12 year old boys.

"Hi Adam!" Andrea's greetings were always full of energy and a radiant smile that could light up the darkest room. Adam returned the smile, looked at Billy, waved goodbye to him and then took Andrea's hand.

"Oh Adam, I missed you so much this week. I couldn't wait to get here to see you!" Andrea told him. "Adam, before we go outside to the sunroom I want you to know that I brought a friend to meet you. He is really nice and he also wants to be your friend. Adam, is this okay with you?"

Adam gripped Andrea's hand harder and nodded. Andrea got the message, "Will you protect me?"

"Adam, this is my friend Brian."

"Hi Adam!"

Brian seemed to be a natural around children, which came as a total surprise to Andrea. She knew he had two children of his own but pictured him as the type that was too busy to be overly involved in their lives. Andrea sat back and listened to Brian talk to Adam about fishing, and about hunting "waskely wrabbits" – sounding a bit like Elmer Fudd which surprisingly got a slight chuckle from everyone and a smile from Adam.

Brian knew his boundaries and was in no way there to try and get anything on the case. Brian needed a fuller understanding of the trauma Adam had gone through, and most importantly, the after effects.

Brian read the doctors reports that Adam was beaten most days on and off for two weeks, poorly fed – if at all – most days, tied back up and left in a dark room, alone, without any hope of escaping. This more than explained the mental shutdown. This was a place of safety for Adam, where he didn't have to live out the nightmares. In many ways it made it seem to Adam like it never happened.

Now that Brian had interacted with Adam he hoped that Adam would never remember the things he'd been through. Brian was even willing to make a deal with Shirley Windsor in order to keep Adam off the stand.

"Adam, you are a very special friend of mine," Brian told him, "and I am most honored to have met you today." Adam stared at Brian with a confused look.

"Brian, simpler," Andrea told him.

"Adam, I want to be your friend. Can I come

back and see you?"

Without a word Adam got up out of his chair and hugged Brian. Andrea began to cry and smile at the same time, while Brian returned the hug.

"Adam, Brian has to go for now, but I am going to stay a little longer. Is that okay with you?"

"Sure," Adam said. This was one of the few words Adam had begun to say lately.

Lunch was cheeseburgers and French fries with grape Kool-Aid. For dessert, cake with ice cream. It was one of the other resident's birthday and his parents brought enough for all fifteen boys, as well as the hungry adults.

On her drive home Andrea felt confident that progress was made today and thanked God for it. She also reminded herself that it had only been eight months, and patience was a must.

As Christmas grew near, Andrea made sure to visit one day during the week and on Saturday. Christmas was a mystery for Andrea since she had no idea what kinds of Christmas Adam had growing up. Andrea decided she would try a little something different. Parents were told not to bring presents to the center because many of the children had no parents or anyone to bring gifts. Since this program was new no one had thought of an outreach program.

After discussing it with the director and finding support from the family members of the other residents, the "okay" was given to bring gifts.

Andrea and two other mothers spear headed the Christmas program. Andrea's church provided a love offering and a local business donated sodas, candy, food, and such for the party. Other family members raised money to bring in gifts suitable for the different ages. The local high school's vocal dimensions group came and sang carols, and the drama class acted out baby Jesus being visited by the wise men from the East.

For being a state run facility it was a miracle of God that they were able to pull this all off. The greatest miracle of the day, however, was the laughter that was heard from children who hadn't said a word in months. If you had been there you would have forgotten that these children were ever sick. Andrea stood back in a corner of the room as tears of joy flowed from her eyes. She looked up to heaven and whispered, "Father, thank You for this miracle."

Over the next several months Brian made a point to visit Adam twice a month. On one visit he even introduced Adam to his own children.

Adam's progress was becoming measureable to both Andrea and the doctors.

Adam began to talk in full sentences one afternoon just prior to his thirteenth birthday. As excited as the staff was they took no sudden action, but kept monitoring Adam's activities. The purpose was to allow Adam to progress naturally out of the shutdown. The doctors feared that too much sudden questioning could trigger a setback. Both Andrea and Brian were instructed to not bring up the past. If Adam should begin to talk about it, they were told to get a doctor in there a quick as possible to assess the conversation. Everyone involved with Adam was in agreement and in no way wanted to hinder his progress.

Six

The Breakthrough

Andrea continued with her visits and brought books for her and Adam to read together. Celebrating Adam's thirteenth birthday was a highlight for Andrea. It was during his party that Adam informed them that he had never had a party before. This raised a lot of questions in Andrea's mind. It was obvious that Adam didn't remember his twelfth birthday, but was it that he *never* had birthday parties before, or were the memories of them just gone?

Andrea informed the staff of Adam's statement and was told that they would investigate it further and let her know what they found out.

During one of the counseling sessions, a therapist made a statement about her upcoming birthday – not that she liked getting older but that she liked the presents she would get. This was a sly attempt to re-open the subject of birthdays with Adam.

Adam, who was relaxed, said cheerfully, "I had a great thirteenth birthday!"

"Oh really? What kind of presents did you get?"

"I got two books. I like to read," Adam told her.

"Who gave you the books?"

"Ms. Andrea."

"Who is Ms. Andrea, Adam?"

"Umm, a friend. She said she is my friend."

"Well Adam, I can almost remember my thirteenth birthday, but I really remember my twelfth birthday."

Adam stared at the therapist as if to be searching his mind for something.

"Adam, what are you thinking about?"

"Umm, I can't seem to remember my twelfth birthday. Is that bad?"

"No, not bad. As I said, I can barely remember my thirteenth birthday, but I do remember my twelfth. Say, maybe you can remember your eleventh birthday?"

Adam thought for a few minutes as the therapist wrote some notes. "Well, I didn't have a party or anything like that."

"Okay, what did you do?"

"I worked!"

"Wow, I'm impressed. What does an eleven year old do for work?"

"My sister and me, we cleaned and…well, we did inside chores because it was so hot."

"So you cleaned your house for your mom?"

"No, cleaned other peoples' houses for money."

"Now I'm really impressed!"

Adam sat up a little straighter in his chair and smiled big. "Well, momma wasn't around much. So me and my sister…we worked to make extra money."

Adam's voice began to soften and trail off as the smile went away.

"Adam, are you okay?"

"Umm…yeah, sure. But I don't feel much like talking right now."

"No problem. What would you like to do?"

"I want to go play with Billy!"

"Okay, go ahead. I will see you in a few days."

The therapist immediately informed the doctor of Adam's apparent memory prior to his blackout. The doctor called Andrea as promised.

"It appears as though Adam may have some triggered memories, induced by the questions asked concerning birthdays. However, it also seems that there may be no memory of things that occurred during the black out. So Ms. Miller, it could be that Adam came out of his blackout prior to this discovery because he remembers you."

"This is great news doctor!" Andrea said.

"Yes, it certainly is, but we must proceed cautiously. Too much too soon can trigger a set-back."

"Of course; I understand. What, or rather how should I talk with him?"

"Just let him talk, and try not to do anything out of the ordinary during your visit with him."

"I get it… be patient. These things take time."

"I couldn't have said it better myself Ms. Miller."

"Thank you, doctor. Thank you very much for calling."

"You're welcome. Goodbye."

"Goodbye."

Andrea immediately thanked God for this gift, and even asked for patience just to be sure she had plenty to get through what laid ahead. Of course she also prayed for Adam to be healed.

Andrea was the one to tell Brian of Adam's progress. An even bigger shock came from Brian.

"Andrea, my office is seriously considering offering Shirley Windsor a plea bargain. I just couldn't imagine having to put Adam on the stand to relive any of his trauma. I have really grown attached to him and I don't want to see him hurt."

"Brian, that is the most empathetic thing you have ever said."

"It's going to be tricky," Brian said, trying not to blush, "Her attorney is no slouch. I wanted to hire him sometime back to work for the "good guys", Brian said with a chuckle.

"Umhmm, go on Brian."

"Well, Andrea, the man knows his stuff and he doesn't care what his client has done, he is going to look out for them. I can see him going to private practice pretty soon... Anyway, I know he doesn't like the True Bill on the 'Especially Aggravated Kidnapping'. Just the mention of it turns him white as a ghost."

"Andrea, let's move on. What do you think about Adam's sudden recovery?"

"Well, I don't know that it is so sudden just because he remembers me. How recent that memory is we aren't sure. Maybe when I visit tomorrow I can get an idea. Brian, the doctor cautioned me again and now I'm reminding you – we can't push him, okay?"

"Of course Andrea. For me it's better left alone. Call me, Andrea, and let me know how it is with him."

"Of course Brian. Goodbye."

"Goodbye."

• • • • •

Two more months went by before the real analysis of Adam Windsor came out. In extensive interviews Adam divulged the beatings, abandonments, the fights his parents had, his daddy leaving and not coming back, the strange men who came to the house, not knowing where his momma worked, her drunkenness, Tina being sick, Tina dying in his arms, and seeing her in the casket.

Andrea and Brian were both invited to the clinical staff meeting concerning Adam's recovery. Andrea cried when the truth of Adam's and Tina's childhood was revealed, while Brian sat speechless, shaking his head in disbelief. It was also apparent, at least for the time being, that Adam would not or could not remember beyond seeing Tina in the casket and asking to leave the funeral. In light of this the doctors were reluctant to try any other methods to induce Adam to remember anything during the blackout. Brian made it clear that his office wouldn't pursue putting Adam on the stand. Likewise, Andrea and DCFS wouldn't pursue it either.

Andrea and Brian knew they each had a lot of work ahead of them now that there were decisions to be made. The past year and a half was spent waiting for Adam to come out of his catatonic state in order to know for sure what he did or didn't remember.

Andrea was now going to have to go to work on finding Adam a home. Because of her personal involvement this would be no easy task. Her standards, compared to what foster care is really like, would not be an easy match.

Likewise, on his drive back from the hospital, Brian was in turmoil over the plea bargain offer to Shirley Windsor. His really big concern was that she might insist on a trial. Brian had seen it before. The parent would want to use intimidation to throw off the child's testimony.

Andrea knew the power of prayer and had already begun to see the Lord's hand at work. It was something Brian would have to learn, and learn quickly.

The weekend passed quickly as Andrea went through files and locations of foster homes. Brian searched case law and his own conscience.

Early Monday morning Andrea showed up unexpectedly at Brian's office. "Andrea...surprised to see you here," Brian said half inquisitively.

"Brian, I want to hear it from you first. What do you think will be the plea bargain?"

"Come in my office. We don't need to discuss it out here."

"Andrea, I have been really troubled and I can't seem to arrive at a decision. I'm confused."

"Brian, it sounds to me like you don't have any peace about it."

"Well, that's true."

"It could also mean something is blocking you."

"Huh?"

"Brian, the apostle Paul wrote that "We don't fight against flesh and blood, but against the rulers, against the authorities, against the world powers of this darkness, against the spiritual forces of evil in the heavens" (Eph. 6:12).

"In other words, Brian, you're trying to fight against an invisible stronghold that doesn't want Shirley Windsor in prison, but *does* want Adam destroyed."

Brian kept quiet for a few minutes soaking in what Andrea had just told him.

"What am I supposed to do Andrea?"

"Pray. I mean really pray! Pray for wisdom. James wrote, "Now if any of you lacks wisdom, he should ask God, who gives to all generously...But let him ask in faith without doubting..." (James 1:5-6).

"Andrea, without doubting?"

That was Brian's whole concern. Did he believe

that God was interested in Adam's case? He never once spiritualized his cases or decisions concerning them.

Andrea had an answer, "Brian, in the Bible I think in Mark, Jesus was confronted by a man whose son was demon possessed. In fact the disciples that were there before Jesus arrived could not cast out the demon. So the man asked Jesus, "If you can do anything, have compassion on us and help us."

"Of course Jesus answered, "If you can? Everything is possible to the one who believes." Then the father of the boy fell down at Jesus' feet and looking up with tears in his eyes said, "I do believe, but help my unbelief."

"God knows our limitations, but He is eager to jump in and help our unbelief. Brian, even the best of Jesus' disciples struggled with faith at one time or another - sometimes a lot!"

"So you mean I don't have to have perfect faith in order to seek God's will?"

"Of course not Brian. Jesus is the only perfect one. And what He wants is for us to trust *His* ability, not ours."

"Well, Andrea, He certainly is able. Hmm, you know, you sure have broken down the confusion I have had for years about not being good enough or strong enough to ask God to get involved. Honestly Andrea, I kinda thought we were alone down here at times, and quite frankly had to do the best we could."

"Brian, don't feel bad about that. You're not the first or the last to think that way. Actually Brian, let me show you here in the Bible how Paul handled human weakness. Here it is in 2 Corinthians 12. Paul had been taken up into the 3rd heaven and shown, as well as heard, some incredibly awesome things by Jesus. But so that he wouldn't boast in himself as being superior to any other man, Satan was permitted to torment him, kinda like you are being tormented. So Paul pleaded to have it stopped, but Jesus told him that "His grace was sufficient". See, here Jesus had responded to Paul's plea. Paul quotes Jesus in saying, "My grace is sufficient for you, for power is perfected in weakness. Now look at what Paul says, "Therefore, I will most gladly boast all the more about my weaknesses so that Christ's power may reside in me" (v. 9).

"See, Brian, it is better to be weak. Here is a great saying to live by that I learned from a pastor friend of mine – "I can't, You can, and I will let You!"

"So Andrea...what you are telling me is, get out of the way and let Jesus do it."

"You got it, Brian. And it all starts with prayer!"

Brian and Andrea prayed right there in his office for the Lord to tear down the stronghold, release Himself and let His will be done.

After praying, Brian and Andrea both had tears running down their faces. Brian told Andrea he was going to call a meeting with his staff and create the deal that the Lord would show him.

Andrea left confident that Jesus was very much in control and said another prayer for Brian and the team.

At the same time the psychiatric team at the State Mental Hospital continued to work with Adam in order to strengthen him and buy Adam some much needed time to find the proper home.

Seven

The Deal

Brian pulled together his team, comprised of an excellent trial lawyer, a phenomenal researcher-lawyer, his lead investigator - who could find anything, and his trusty paralegal who was very astute and accurate. For a small town D.A.'s office Brian could put them up against the best in the country.

It was at this meeting that Brian expressed for the first time on this one and a half year old case that he wanted a Plea Bargain for Shirley Windsor. "Guys, I know I was adamant about not giving in and offering a deal but I have changed my mind. I am convinced that Adam doesn't need any more trauma in his life. And making him relive those horrible days... well, it would do reprehensible damage – that is, if Adam can remember them. Either way, I'm not willing to risk it."

There came a noticeable sigh of relief from among the team members.

"Well Brian, I agree," responded the lead investigator, Mac Johnson. "We have plenty of physical evidence," he continued.

"Brian, what are you considering?" Came the general question from the team.

"I feel the defense attorney is posturing to go trial because the delays have mostly been on our part. However, he turns white as a ghost when I tell him the charge we will prosecute for is 'Especially Aggravated Kidnapping'. He knows if he loses, his client could easily get the max of 25 years. Of course he also risks the judge enhancing the time due to the seriousness of the offense and taking it to 60 years, which would be life. Of course I'm posturing a little as if Adam was to remember and testify."

"Knowing all of this I was considering 'Aggravated Child Abuse and Neglect', which is still a "B" class felony and carries an 8-12 year sentence. It is not very likely that the judge would enhance that one – of course I could throw in that we ask the judge *not* to enhance."

"Brian, I have to ask," said Andy the researcher, "what if the defense says no?"

"Well, let's just say I have information that assures me the deal will be accepted," Brian's face lit up as he responded. He knew in his heart that God was in control.

"Well you're the boss," was Mac's response. And then a resounding "yes" followed from the others.

"Guys, here's what I want to do. First, gather all the boxes of evidence, notes, and anything else we have on the Shirley Windsor case and stack it against the back wall of the small conference room. The small room will give the illusion of "less is more." Then

Mac, I want you to spend the next couple of days kicking up some dust. I want the Public Defender's office to notice some activity on the case. Amanda, get me the up-to-date judges' schedules in case we need to move the case to another judge."

"David, as the trial lawyer and spokesperson for this case, throw a little bone to the media that Adam is now being interviewed. And Andy, write this deal so that it is air tight, and have it on my desk no later than Thursday. On Friday I will call Tim Sutton personally and ask him to come over here so I can present the deal. I'm confident guys, come Monday afternoon, this will all be over."

The dust kicking and noise making had Tim Sutton meeting with his client within 36 hours.

"Shirley, as your attorney I must advise you that if Mr. Smith pursues a trial he will go after the conviction of 'Especially Aggravated Kidnapping', which as we have discussed before, is a class "A" felony and carries a 25 year max – even for a first time offender. And I'm sure Mr. Miller will get into your character and bring out the two arrests for prostitution."

"Well Mr. Hotshot-lawyer-with-all-the-answers, what do you think we should do?"

"Ms. Windsor, I'm sure you're angry and all, but taking it out on me or displaying it in court won't help you a bit. Also, it isn't 'we', it's what *you* should do."

"Well, okay then…Mr. Sutton, what should I

do?"

"With your permission Ms. Windsor, let me ask the D.A.'s office what they would consider on a plea bargain. They might kick out the 'Especially Aggravated Kidnapping' and shoot for one of the lower charges. That could save you 13 years of prison life."

"Well I don't recall what the other charges are."

"The next charge is 'Aggravated Child Abuse and Neglect'. That's a "B" class felony and carries an 8-12 year sentence. Then they also have filed Desertion and non-support, which is an "E" class felony and carries 1-2 years. If they didn't drop it, they would probably offer it as a concurrent sentence. No extra time but it would be on your record."

"Well Mr. Sutton, tell them I will take the abuse charge at 8 years and drop the other two all together!"

"Ms. Windsor, it doesn't work that way. I know all the smack talk and jailhouse lawyering you have heard but those old heads are just spitting in the wind. Let me handle this the right way. Believe me, I know Brian Smith well and he isn't a game player."

Tim Sutton beat Brian to the call. Just as Brian was looking over the small conference room and thinking to himself about how much material had been gathered concerning the Shirley Windsor case Amanda interrupted, "Brian, Tim Sutton is on line two. He would like to speak with you."

Brian put on his game face, sat down at his desk and before picking up the receiver, prayed to God that His will be done.

"Good morning, Tim. How are you?"

"Well, not bad. The Bears look good for this season. Hope to go to a few games before it gets too cold. How are you, Brian?"

"Busy, and the kids are growing up faster that I can keep up with. So Tim, how can I help you?"

"Brian, I want to get together and talk about the Shirley Windsor case."

Brian paused, mostly for dramatics – and to not seem too eager.

"Let me see here…my schedule is kind of tight. I tell you what Tim…come here to my office at noon."

"Noon…No problem, Brian. I'll see you then."

One last meeting with the team and Brian was ready to meet with Tim Sutton.

At noon sharp Tim Sutton appeared at the receptionist's desk of Brian Smith. Amanda escorted Tim down the carpeted hallway to Conference Room B. Tim was met there by Brian, Mac, David, and Andy.

"Wow, Brian, I didn't come to start a war. What's with all the weight?"

"Tim it is as much for your good as mine that we have witnesses. This isn't some D.U.I. case that gets bantered around in the court hallways."

"Yeah, you're right."

"Well Tim, you called this meeting. What's on your mind?" Brian was setting the "no game playing" attitude and platform which he was very well known for.

"My client has grown somewhat of a conscience and I would like to say it is for Adam's benefit, but I can't. I believe it is self-preservation. With that being said, Brian, what kind of a deal would you consider? Of course no trial would save a lot of taxpayer money."

"Tim, I am confident that the tax payers couldn't care less about the cost. This case is about a child who was beat and tied up and left for dead." Brian could have gone on but in reality he was preaching to the wrong person so he relented.

"Tim…" Brian paused again and looked over at all the boxes stacked along the conference room back wall. then made direct eye contact with each team member. "The Bible tells us not to judge outsiders and that God is the Righteous and Just Judge of all people. 'Vengeance is Mine, sayeth the Lord, I will repay' (Hebrews 10:30). The only deal we will consider is Aggravated Child Abuse and Neglect, and Shirley Windsor must do the max. Trust me, Counselor, that it is a gift to your client. But most importantly it is a reprieve to young Adam Windsor, from having to re-live the trauma all over again."

No one on the team flinched at Brian's statement which would lead one to think Adam was ready to testify. Tim shifted his weight in an attempt not to appear uncomfortable. Tim was in his own right a formidable attorney, but even he understood the magnitude and public sentiment surrounding this case.

"Thank you, Brian, for your generosity. I will do my best to present it to my client as to being in her best interest."

This is where it gets sticky. Attorneys can make recommendations, answer questions pertaining to law, and clarify facts – things of this nature, but they cannot make the decision or force their clients to make the decision that they would prefer. The client must choose for themselves.

With that said, all the formalities of social etiquette where performed and Tim left.

Still gathered in the small conference room the entire team breathed a sigh of relief.

"Good job boss, good job!" Mac was enthusiastic and loved to see a pro at work. Then came more accolades of congratulations.

"Thank you all for your support, but I want you to know that unlike many cases in the past, this time I sought God for His will to be done. And from now on, both in my job and in my home, God will be the one who runs the show. I couldn't have done it without Him, and I'm afraid to say that little Adam would have been traumatized all over again. I don't know how many of you believe in Christ, but let me tell you "He *is* the Way, the Truth, and the Life" (John 14:6).

"I was very troubled and couldn't get a handle

on this case. Whenever I tried I was blocked. A very good friend of mine told me that the Devil himself was blocking me and causing the problems. After seeing in the Bible where we don't fight flesh and blood, but evil spirits, I was convinced in my heart that only through Christ could the battle in this life be won."

"I also learned that even though we have problems in this world we are to be courageous because Jesus has overcome this world. So after years of fighting by myself, I surrendered my life to Jesus and now He fights for me. Now I have joy and peace deep inside of me that no power can take from me. I am committed to allowing Jesus to run my life entirely."

Amanda had tears running down her face, "Brian, I have not been following the Lord the way I used to. I'm sure that's why my marriage is a mess and I seem troubled a lot. In fact I have been using work as a place to hide my emotions and to distract me from my problems. I want to come back to Him. He is really the only way to live." The tear ducts opened like Niagara Falls as Amanda bowed her head and sobbed.

Mac looked at Brian with tears in his eyes and said, "How can I know this Jesus you are telling us about? I always thought that God was just some invisible force that would destroy the world someday, and I guessed that if you were good enough, you would go to a place called heaven. If not, then hell, and be tortured forever."

Brian opened his briefcase and took out his Bible.

"Mac, look here in John chapter 3, verse 16 and 17, "For God loved the world in this way: He gave His one and only Son, so that everyone who believes in Him will not perish but have eternal life. For God did not send His Son into the world that He might condemn the world, but that the world might be saved through Him."

"See Mac, God loves us and wants us to turn away from the way we are, turn to Him, and be saved. It isn't about how good or bad we are. Romans 3:23 says that all have sinned and fallen short of the glory of God."

"But while we were still helpless (meaning that we couldn't save ourselves), at the appointed moment, Christ died for the ungodly' (Romans 5:6). And then look here. 'But God proves His own love for us in that while we were still sinners Christ died for us' (Romans 5:8)".

"Here in Romans 10 it says, 'If you confess with your mouth, "Jesus is Lord," and believe in your heart that God raised Him from the dead, you will be saved. With the heart one believes, resulting in righteousness, and with the mouth one confesses, resulting in salvation' (v. 9-10)".

"I know now, Brian, that I need a savior…I can't save myself from the sins I have committed."

Brian led Mac to the Lord in a prayer of salvation. Then he led Amanda, David, and Andy in a
prayer of rededication as they chose to seek the Lord
as their Lord and to surrender their lives to Him.

• • • • •

Tim Sutton stopped by his supervisors office
to inform him of the plea bargain offered by Brian
Smith. Tim also did a little fast talking to convince
his boss that this was a final offer. With an "okay"
from the boss Tim proceeded to the County jail to
meet with Shirley Windsor.

"Ms. Windsor, I have good news."

"I get to leave now?" Shirley said as she lit up
a cigarette.

"Ms. Windsor…" Tim was determined to blow
off the attitude and get to the point. "The D.A. has
offered 'Aggravated Child Abuse and Neglect', which
means you will be sentenced to 12 years, and with
good days you could be out in 9."

"Is that the best you can do?"

"Ms. Windsor, that's the best you're going to get.
Take it or leave it. This D.A. isn't playing games with
you and he has the public sentiment to back it up. I
suggest you give it some serious thought and stop
listening to those old hags in your cell block before
you mess around and get life."

"Life?! What?! Who said anything about life??"

"Ms. Windsor, I did some research before

coming here. If the judge decides to enhance the sentencing to the severity, which by the way the law allows him to do, he can max a class A felony out to 60 years. Ms. Windsor, next year is an election year. That's only a month or so away and this will make for a great campaign."

Tim stood up and gathered his brief case to leave, "Don't take too long. Mr. Smith will push hard for a trial date now."

"Hold on! Hold on. Are you sure that there's no funny stuff or surprises?"

"I'm sure. Mr. Smith doesn't play games like that."

"Okay, I'll take the deal. When can we get to the judge and get it over with?"

"I'm sure it will be soon - everyone wants this case over with. I'll let you know when I get the date.

• • • • •

The date was set for Tuesday, November 21st, at 11:45 am., only a few weeks after Ms. Windsor agreed to the deal. Once Ms. Windsor signed the plea bargain she was remanded to the custody of the Illinois Dept. of Corrections.

Brian was congratulated by everyone – including the public.

"Well, how do you feel now, Mr. D.A?" Andrea asked once the courtroom cleared.

"I feel really at peace about it all. But you know, I wasn't expecting the public to be so agreeable."

"Brian, I am convinced that since you honored God and allowed Him to work it according to His will, He gave you favor. That's one of the blessings of being hooked up with the Almighty."

"Hey Andrea, I have to run, but remind me to tell you what happened in my office a couple of weeks back."

"Yeah, sure Brian…I'll see you."

Andrea's thoughts drifted off to Adam and how God spared that child the horror of testifying, and also that the time Adam could stay in special care was running out. With a sigh Andrea whispered, "Lord Jesus, I trust that you will find the right home for Adam. And thank You for today. Amen."

Eight

A Home For Adam

Andrea had a fitful night of sleep. 'The Deal' that ended one saga of young Adam's life was over, but what lay ahead certainly remained a mystery. Andrea was trusting the Lord to provide a good and stable home for Adam but as with many of us, life got the best of her.

She rolled over and eyed the bright red numbers of her digital clock "5am! Ughhhh! No sense lying here tossing and turning. Do something, Andrea."

Andrea had no problem giving herself a little pep talk once in a while. She humored herself, "Well, at least I'm not answering myself."

Andrea splashed some water on her face, changed into her sweatpants and sweatshirt, put on her running shoes and got herself moving. Andrea enjoyed running and now, after a couple years of it, she was up to 6 miles a day. Not only did she like the health benefits, she knew how cleansing it was to her mind. Most importantly, though, she used this as her private prayer time. Getting close to God was Andrea's number one goal in life. She often prayed, "Lord Jesus, please keep drawing me closer to you. I can't do anything without you." And she knew all too well that it was the Lord's will that must be done concerning Adam.

After she took a shower Andrea made herself comfortable in her oversized living room chair and began to review the latest foster parents who had applied for Adam.

Adam's situation was very different since so very little was known about what damage the blackout may have caused. The doctors at the center where Adam was housed used this, and other research needs, to keep Adam until Andrea and her office could find a good home for him.

Andrea was aware of the separation of Church and State so she knew she couldn't base her decision solely on her desire to place him in a Christian home. However, she did make a point to do a little fishing during the interviews. One of her more clever ploys was to ask about Christmas. Now that is was the Christmas season Andrea would describe how she loves Christmas and why – of course she was focused on the birth of the Lord Jesus and would wait for the interviewees response. Andrea wasn't too surprised to find that a little less than half of the interviewees responded in kind.

Nonetheless, energized by her prayer-run Andrea plowed on, being critical of every application she read. Andrea was so intense in her thoughts that she was startled when her phone rang.

"Hello…Hey mom…Oh, no I didn't forget our

lunch date…11:30? Yep, I'll be there…Love you too mom."

Andrea truly enjoyed spending time with her mother. Andrea knew full well what the power of forgiveness could do to a relationship. And her forgiving her mother by the strength of the Lord was a testimony she loved to share.

The morning flew by as Andrea thoroughly reviewed the twenty applications. Andrea selected five to call on Monday. Now it was time to meet mom for lunch.

During lunch Andrea gave her mom a full update on Adam's situation and the great recovery he was making. Andrea mentioned that she wouldn't be at worship in the morning at their family church because she was going to attend worship at the hospital with Adam and the other children. Andrea had been selected to teach the children about salvation through faith in Jesus, who forgives us of all our sins. This in itself was a miracle from God.

"The rule – as it goes – says we can't force anyone to attend the worship service, and as long as they are minors their parents or guardians can block them from the service," Andrea explained to her mom. "To this date no one has objected.

Andrea knew that in crisis situations people who never attend church often will - such as in natural disasters or times of war. The Specialty Care Unit at the State Mental Hospital is a crisis center and the parents know it.

At the close of the service one 14 year old boy asked Jesus to forgive him and be his Lord. To Andrea's disappointment Adam didn't make a move. Andrea wasn't sure if Adam understood the message of salvation. What happened next shocked the 'always prepared' Andrea Miller.

At lunch Adam remained quiet and seemed to be adrift in his thoughts – even somewhat tense. Andrea was busy with the many questions some of the children were asking and thought it best to allow Adam his space.

The lunch crowd broke up and Andrea walked with Adam to the sunroom. Adam liked the sunroom because of all the windows that let light in. Adam sat down and stared out, watching as a light snow began to fall.

Without turning to look at Andrea, Adam asked a most profound and unexpected question.

"Andrea, you said that God created all things, including us humans and that He loves us more than we could ever understand…then tell me, why did he let my sister die?"

Before Andrea could respond, Adam went on. "And how come He would let my momma beat me?? Why am I hurting so bad?" Adam's fists were clinched and his jaw was tense.

Amid the shock of Adam's questions Andrea feverishly began to search her memory bank for a message she may have heard or even something in her own experience that could give her an answer.

Several minutes passed as Andrea prayed to God to give her the insight and the words to say. "Lord, please touch his little heart, for only You can heal."

"Adam, it's true that God loves us. In fact "God is love" (1 John 4:8,16). It is a love beyond what we can fully understand, but it isn't beyond our being able to experience it. See, what happens is that when people are angry and upset, or even bitter, they can't feel God's love.

"Adam, way back in the beginning, when God created man, He made them perfectly. In fact Adam, for a long time they didn't do anything wrong. Have you ever done anything bad or wrong, Adam?"

Adam paused a minute, then told Andrea how he'd gotten so mad at Tina that he yelled at her and made her cry.

"Okay then, so you felt bad, right?"

"Yes, I sure did feel bad. I did say I was sorry, though."

"I'm glad for that, and so Tina felt better then?"

"Yep. She said she knew I didn't mean it."

"Well guess what? God didn't mean for bad things to happen either. See, God made Adam and Eve, a man and woman, and placed them in paradise, a garden God made especially for us called Eden. I said "for us" because they had babies and those babies grew up and had more kids and soon populated the earth. It wasn't just so the earth would be populated, though, more importantly God wanted lots of children."

"Now God gave Adam and Eve the ability to choose – you know, to make their own choices. If He hadn't, well, then they would have been like puppets on strings, doing only what their master wanted. But God wanted real life people to love Him as a Father, not a master. So God even visited them and walked with them in the "cool of the day", the Bible says. Oh it must have been wonderful."

"But something tragic happened. God gave them one rule. Adam, you know why there are rules, right?"

"Sure, to keep people from getting hurt, or something like that."

"Good Adam, that's right. Well, God made a rule. He told them "You are free to eat from any tree in the garden; but you must not eat from the tree of the knowledge of good and evil, for when you eat from it you will certainly die." (Genesis 2:16-17)

"For a long time they didn't touch it or even go near it. Then the Devil came along disguised as a beautiful serpent. The Bible even tells us that the serpent was the "most cunning of all the wild animals" – meaning he was a liar and very tricky. He tricked the woman Eve into eating the fruit from that tree God said not to, and then she gave some to her husband Adam, and he ate it also.

"So Adam, what they did was wrong, right?"

"Yeah, they did something they were told not to do."

"That's right, and that is what we call sin."

"What happened to them, Andrea? Did they die like Tina did?"

"Not at that moment, no. But what happened is that they died spiritually and lost the perfect relationship that they had with God. See, God planned for them to live forever with Him. But since they disobeyed, God limited their days as to how long they could live in the flesh, and then sent them out of the garden to work for their food."

"Now because of their disobedience sin entered the world. The Bible tells us in Romans Chapter 5, "Therefore, just as sin entered the world through one man, and death through sin, in this way death spread to all men, because all sinned."

"So the perfect world that God intended for us to live in was destroyed because Adam and Eve listened to the Devil."

"Andrea, you mean it's the Devil's fault that Tina died?"

"Yes! That's it exactly. God never intended for Tina or anyone else to die. And Adam, the best news is that God made a way for all of us to come back to Him and live forever with Him in paradise when our work here on earth is through."

"For God so loved the world that He gave His

one and only Son so that everyone who believes in Him will not perish but have eternal life" (John 3:16).

"Jesus Christ died on the cross, was buried, and was raised to life again on the third day to prove God's love for us. Now by faith – which means that I believe even though I can't see – by faith in Jesus, the penalty for sin – which is death – is paid for by Jesus' death. So we are no longer judged for what we did in our old sinful selves – which was to reject God and do our life the way we wanted to. Now we are new creatures in Christ Jesus. You see, Jesus comes to live in you – actually inside of you, by His Spirit the Holy Spirit, who then will guide you every step of the way for the rest of your life."

"And Adam…Jesus heals those who are angry, confused, hurting, and sad, because He loves us so much."

Andrea paused to take in all she said knowing that God had given it to her and prayed that God would work in Adam's heart.

Andrea opened her eyes from prayer and looked at Adam. For the first time since the blackout Adam had tears running down his face.

Adam got out of his seat and collapsed in Andrea's arms, sobbing as if the weight of the world was being lifted from him. Andrea held him tight and cried with him.

After a few minutes Adam raised up, "Andrea, I want Jesus…I want Jesus to be my Lord and Savior."

Andrea led Adam in a prayer of salvation.

"Andrea, I feel so much better now. I know Jesus has healed me – it's like I heard Him tell me so."

"Andrea...I do have another question."

"Of course Adam, what is it?"

"What happened to Tina? I mean, do you think she is in heaven?"

"Adam, I don't *think* – and I'm not guessing ... I *know* she is. Adam, because Tina wasn't old enough to know she needed to choose God, He chose her."

"He really does love us doesn't He, Andrea?"

"Yes Adam, He certainly does."

With that Andrea and Adam walked hand in hand back to the central unit. Visiting hours were over.

Once in her car Andrea sat there and cried tears of release and joy, and praised to God for His great grace and mercy. She stood once again at the foot of the cross, looked up and said, "Thank You! I love You with all my heart!"

As Andrea drove home she could sense God's loving presence with her. The view from the rearview mirror was just another reminder of God's awesome creative beauty. The sun was setting with clouds that created streams of light causing the snow blowing about in the wind to glisten like diamonds.

Andrea was totally convinced that God was in control of Adam's life. Therefore the restlessness in her mind and spirit from the day before melted away like snow melting in the early spring sun.

Andrea arrived home and went into the house by way of the garage entrance into the kitchen. Before she even turned on the light she noticed the red light blinking on her answering machine, indicating that she had a message.

After Andrea turned on the light she sat her purse and keys on the table and made her way to the machine, all along thinking that her mother must have called to see how the worship service was at the State Mental Hospital.

Andrea was tired and half thought of not playing the message, knowing she could pacify her mother in the morning…

"Oh, I should just listen and call her. Today was a great day, with some very good news."

"You have one message," came the robotic voice as Andrea pushed the play button. "Hi Andrea, this is Brian Smith. My wife Charlotte and I need to talk with you as soon as you get this message. Please call – even if it's late. The number is 555-1382. Thank you. Click." Beeep.

A thousand and one horrors immediately raced through Andrea's mind as she scrambled for a pen and paper to write down his number.

"Brian calling me at home??...on a Sunday… what could be so urgent? Maybe Shirley Windsor escaped…oh don't be silly Andrea. Besides, he said… gosh I need to clean out this drawer. Can't find a thing…that he and his wife want to talk…Here we go 5-5-5-1-3-8-2."

Andrea grabbed the wall mounted phone, picking up the receiver that hung just above the answering machine next to the kitchen cabinets, and dialed Brian's number.

"Hello, Smith residence."

"Hello, my name is Andrea Miller. May I speak to Brian Smith?"

"Daaad! Phone!"

Andrea had to move the phone away from her ear due to the blast that must have carried through the entire house.

"Hello, this is Brian."

"Brian, it's Andrea. I called as soon as I got home."

"Andrea! Great, thank you so much!"

Andrea was taken back by Brian's enthusiasm. "Well Brian, I can't remember the last time someone was so happy to hear from me – occupational hazard, you know?"

"I sure do, Andrea, and I am sorry to call on a Sunday, but Charlotte and I must talk with you."

"No problem, when?"

"How about in thirty minutes…at the dinner on 8th Ave and Charleston – unless you are busy?"

"No, no, not too busy." Andrea had made her career her life so she had become accustomed to not having lots of social events or happenings. And she didn't mind a bit.

"Brian, the suspense is killing me. What's so urgent?" Andrea had a very noticeable smile in her voice and was catching Brian's excitement.

"I won't say on the phone – habit I guess. Plus Charlotte wants to be a part of this."

"Okay then, I'll be there in thirty."

Andrea hung up the phone and went to freshen up. She changed into some jeans and a sweatshirt. Andrea sat on the foot of her bed. She just couldn't imagine what Brian and his wife wanted with her. It was 7:35 and it only took 10 minutes to get there so Andrea finished dressing and then called her mother. She wanted to tell her the exciting news about the two boys who gave their lives to Jesus. Of course she told her all about Adam as well.

"Mom, hey, I've got to run. Brian Smith and his wife Charlotte need to see me tonight at the Rauch diner....I'm not sure yet, he just sounded excited and said that both of them needed to see me.....Of course Mother, I will tell you – if it isn't work related and confidential, you know.....I will, love you too. Tell dad I love him too. Goodbye."

Andrea took a short cut, passing the Catholic Church and the R.C. Bottling plant. Dumping out onto north street she turned left down main street, went over the via dock and took a right on 8th street. She drove down half a block and parked right in front.

"Andrea!" Brian hollered from the back left booth, waving enthusiastically.

"Hi Charlotte! Hi Brian!" Andrea and the Smiths greeted warmly.

Becky, a college student whose parents owned the restaurant, greeted Andrea with hot coffee and a menu.

"Thank you, Becky. How's school?"

"Great, but calculus is a drag. I'll finish my undergraduate in May and then head to the Chicago law school."

Brian smiled as though he was the inspiration Becky used to go into law. "Criminal law, right Becky?"

"No, I really want contract law. I'm not much about being in front of grumpy judges."

Everyone laughed as Becky smiled and walked away.

"Okay you two, no formalities. We've known each other since high school. What gives?"

Charlotte was the one to break the news. "Andrea, Brian and I would like to give Adam a home!"

You could have heard a pin drop as Andrea stared into the wide open eyes of Charlotte and Brian, trying to comprehend what Charlotte had just said.

"And not only that…we would like to adopt Adam, if he wants that."

Andrea did the best she could to control the flood of emotions that were suddenly over-taking her. She could hardly speak. "But when?... I mean what...what brought this on?"

"Andrea, ever since that morning in my office when you led me back to the Lord, well, my whole life began to change. And now over these last few months, the Lord...well, He's been doing something in my family as well. See, Charlotte and I, we always wanted 3,4 or even 5 children, but after Alex was born Charlotte wasn't able to carry any more children. Now, nine years later, it has been laid on our hearts to adopt. We understand, though, if Adam doesn't want to be adopted. We would still like to be his foster parents at least."

Andrea sat there with tears of joy streaming down her face and began to softly thank Jesus.

"Andrea...," Charlotte lowered her voice and with a pleading look on her face asked, "What would be our chances to have Adam live with us?"

Andrea dried her eyes and cleared her voice. "No problem, consider it done."

"God gave us His Son," Andrea continued, "and still, even in our weakness, keeps giving us more. I am just overwhelmed. I had no idea how He was going to provide – He is never late or short on kindness. Thank you Lord Jesus. Thank you."

With that the three held hands and bowed their heads while Brian led them in a prayer of thanksgiving.

Andrea composed herself and gave Brian and Charlotte a short list of "must-haves" for foster care, then laid out the plan.

"First things first…How long will it take for you to have room for Adam?"

"We have already prepared in faith. He will share a room with Ben."

"Good! Tomorrow I will make a call to Springfield. Tracy Johnson owes me one and we will expedite the paper work. Let's get Adam home for Christmas!" Andrea was in top form now, clicking off procedure as proof of her years of experience.

"Give Adam time to get settled, then approach him about adoption. Since he is 13 and has no relatives, that we know of, he can choose for himself. He has been through a lot so let's be gentle with him and his needs."

"We agree, Andrea!" came a simultaneous response from the Smiths.

"First thing, Charlotte, at like 7am, can you bring me the documents I need?"

"Of course. I know exactly where everything is at."

Andrea commented on Charlotte's almost obsessive compulsive behavior from High School and was now grateful for it. Everyone laughed a moment and relished in the joy that the Lord was at work in their lives.

"Okay then, it's settled. After I have the documents and the paperwork in order, I'll get Brenda to help me. She's got to be the fastest typist in the Midwest. Then I'll have Mr. Thompson sign off. Once I have everything finalized I'll call you."

Everyone was in agreement. The Smiths went home to tell their boys the good news, while Andrea went to her office to pull all the necessary forms and fill them out as far as she could without the Smiths information. Andrea knew it would be futile to go home and rest. She was way too excited, and above all, Adam was more than worth all the effort everyone could put into expediting his move.

By 3pm Monday afternoon Andrea called Charlotte. "Charlotte, hi, it's Andrea. Everything is settled on our end."

"Really?! Oh Andrea, this is wonderful! What next?"

"Well, you and Brian will need to come to the hospital with me tomorrow to sign Adam's release papers and bring him home."

Andrea thought about what she said and wondered if it sounded like adopting a pet from the animal shelter…Not to labor the point, she moved on.

"Charlotte, we should leave by 7am. I will call the doctor when we leave to let him know we are on our way so that they can be ready. Trust me, they know the urgency to find Adam a home and are on standby."

The Smiths pulled into the hospital parking lot with their two boys Ben and Alex, 11 and 9 years old. They were just a few minutes ahead of Andrea.

"Boys, this is Ms. Miller."

Charlotte was now a stay at home mom and taught her children proper etiquette.

"Good morning Ms. Miller. I'm Ben Smith." Ben stuck out his hand all formal like and then Alex followed suit.

"Nice to meet you both. Are you excited?"

"Yes ma'am."

"Ummm, Charlotte? Can I just be Andrea? This ma'am stuff is good and all, but I'm not a ma'am yet."

"Of course, if that's what you want, ma'am."

Everyone laughed at the jest of humor. Not to mention it was a needed break from the nervous tension that everyone was feeling.

"Okay guys, let me go talk with Adam first and break the ice." Andrea was polite but she knew from experience how to handle such delicate news. It just had to be this way.

"No problem, Andrea," Brian answered. "We are here to cooperate."

With that all five of them made their way to the specialty unit and were greeted warmly by the staff. Andrea went to find Adam in the craft area while Mr. and Mrs. Smith received instructions from the clinical psychologist as to what they might encounter with Adam.

Andrea entered the room quietly and observed Adam from behind for just a moment. She paused to thank Jesus for His unending love. "Be with us

Lord. We need you."

"Adam."

"Andrea! Andrea!" Adam ran to Andrea and gave her a big hug. "Hey, it's not Wednesday night – why are you here? I mean, I'm glad to see you!"

"I'm glad to see you too. Say, did you get taller since Sunday?"

"You think so? Maybe it's these new shoes. They're thicker than my old ones. Some people from a church brought all of us new shoes yesterday. They were super nice and we sang Christmas songs and had candy."

"Wow Adam, you sure have had a busy couple of days."

"Yeah I know, I think Jesus planned it. I heard someone say that all good things come from God the Father through Mary so that we could see Him."

"Wow, that's pretty awesome!"

"Sure is."

"Now can I tell you why I'm here, Adam?"

"Sure."

"Okay, come over here and let's sit down."

"Adam, do you know that this place isn't your home to grow up in, right?"

"Yes, the therapist told me that someday I would be well enough to leave and go home. That really confused me."

"Oh? Why?"

"Well, it didn't feel right for one thing…and I

think my mom ran away like my dad did. I mean I've not ever heard of her or seen her since Tina's funeral, so I don't know if I *can* go home."

Andrea really had to pause and get a handle on her thoughts. How she responded to Adam here could set off a relapse or some other drastic result. Andrea prayed, "Lord, You brought the Smiths and me to this point. Please tell me what to say now."

Adam didn't hear the prayer but since Andrea sat real quiet with her eyes closed he thought that's what she was doing.

"Adam, do you want to go home, to the place you used to live?" Andrea's heart was in her throat as she waited for Adam to answer.

"No, I don't want to…You're not gonna send me back there are you?"

"No…no Adam, never. Do you remember Alex and Ben?"

"Yes, Mr. Smith is their daddy. They come and see me quite a bit."

"So do you like them?"

"Sure do. Ben and I, we like a lot of the same things, even though I'm older. And Alex is really funny, like a comedian or something."

"Adam, that's great! Mr. and Mrs. Smith want you to come live with them!"

"Really! Are you sure? No foolin' Andrea?"

"That's right, no foolin'. For real!"

"When?"

"They are here now, if it's alright with you?"

"You mean I can leave today?"

"Yep, that's exactly what I mean."

Well let's go!" Adam said as he grabbed Andrea's hand, practically dragging her to the main unit.

Adam ran to Ben and Alex, jumping up and down in total excitement. High fives were exchanged all around.

"Mr. Smith and ma'am, I am really quite glad that you will let me live with you. I know how to work hard and be responsible. I won't be no problem."

Charlotte knelt down, taking both of Adam's hands into hers, "Adam, we want you to relax and be *you*, have fun and grow to experience life as it comes. There will be plenty of time for you to work and be responsible later. What do you think about that?"

"Well, I would like that too, ma'am."

"Oh, and Adam, you can call me Charlotte or mom - whatever you are comfortable with."

"Yes ma'am, I mean Charlotte." Everyone laughed, including Adam.

With bags packed and final goodbyes to friends and staff, Adam Windsor walked out of the Illinois Hospital for the Mentally Ill Special Care Unit to embark on a whole new life.

Nine

Love God's Way

It was windy and only 10 degrees and the hour was 5am on December 22nd. Adam Windsor stood in his living room looking down on Michigan Avenue from the 8th floor of his condo building. A typical Chicago winter morning, Adam thought, but a very untypical day lay before him.

Adam went back in time to reflect on his life. Some things really stood out to him, such as his parent's divorce, being left by his mother, working to earn extra money to take care of Tina and himself when he was only 9, 10, and 11. Of course the promise he made to Tina to always take care of her. Adam also remembered how Brian and Charlotte helped him to understand that Tina's death wasn't his fault, but the result of a birth defect that destroyed her heart.

Late in high school Adam asked many question about his mom and where she was. Why did Brian and Charlotte open their home to him? Neither Andrea Miller or the Smith family expected that Adam would ever ask about the blackout, but he did.

Adam wanted answers and no one denied him

the truth. And as we all know, sometimes the truth hurts.

Adam swore in his anger that he would never forgive Shirley Windsor. Charlotte pleaded for him to find it in his heart to forgive but Adam wouldn't hear of it.

As it turns out the blackout didn't do away with any of the hurt, pain, sorrow, or anger; it only drove it deep into the inner recesses of his mind.

Adam of course went about his religious duties, such as church attendance, Sunday school, and even taught at a youth camp the summer before college. But none of this brought the deep inner peace Adam wanted.

Adam was smart and graduated ahead of his class by a whole year, which gave him the advantage to land a top notch job. Brown and Brown, a stock brokerage firm, hired Adam on the spot.

Adam applied every ounce of energy he had to climbing the ladder of success. Earning rookie of the year got him the attention of the senior partners.

That was all it took – Adam earned a managing spot at the firm. This of course came with a corner office, his own secretary, and bigger accounts. Adam's income soared to over $200,00 in his third year with the firm and, as they said around the office, "The sky's the limit." Still Adam felt something was wrong in his heart - that something was missing.

Early in December Adam had taken the

weekend off and gone home to visit Brian and Charlotte. Was he in search of something or just going
for a visit? Adam asked himself that question several
times on that two and a half hour drive home.

"What could I be missing?" he thought. "I have
a luxury condo, fancy clothes, fine dining, the Mer-
cedes I always wanted, and lots of friends. And I still
pray for my family and friends. Why do I feel empty?"

Little did Adam know what God had in store
for him that weekend.

Arriving just in time for Charlotte's famous
beef stroganoff and the quiet conversation around
the dinner table gave Adam a much needed break
from his usual late supper and hectic Fridays. Adam
brought Brian and Charlotte up to date on some
new west coast clients that kept him at the office
till 7pm most days. As far as dating, "Nah, just a
few friends to catch a movie or a late supper. No big
deal." Adam didn't feel that dating was an important
part of his life.

"Well, how about church? What are you
involved in?" That was Charlotte's way of checking
up on Adam.

"Well...I've been super busy and usually end up
sleeping in on Sunday."

Charlotte sighed as usual and gave him her "I'm
worried" look. Adam knew that deep down inside his
relationship with the Lord was more distant than an
occasional friend he'd go to a movie with.

Adam quickly changed the subject and started asking them questions. Charlotte talked for a few minutes about the ladies guild at church and their fund raising for a local outreach ministry.

Brian piped in and rattled off how he enjoyed his position as a judge. "Sure is better being on this side of the bench," Brian said with a big smile and a confident air about him.

After dinner and dessert, Adam helped Charlotte clean up – which was a regular habit of his and Charlotte always appreciated it.

"Oh by the way, if I didn't mention it, I am meeting Andrea in the morning. We are going Christmas shopping and then to lunch."

"You mentioned it. I hope you two have a great time."

Adam arrived at Andrea's house at 8am sharp, as agreed.

"Hey sis, you ready?"

"Yep, let me grab my coat."

The two spent the first hour talking and catching up on work and the life each one new as their career.

It was at lunch that Andrea noticed the distant look in Adam's eyes. Andrea probed gently just in case she was wrong, but one thing she knew well were people, and Adam Windsor – she knew him the best.

The years proved to build a strong brother-sister

relationship between the two. And in a lot of unspoken ways Adam knew he owed his very life to Andrea. When Andrea had heard enough of his salesman double-talk she called him out.

"Adam Windsor, out with it!"

"Out with what, Andrea?"

"I know something is eating at you."

Adam knew he was caught. And for a brief moment of time he was glad. He knew something was wrong – why keep hiding?

"Andrea, I feel empty…I don't know why… something seems unsettled."

Andrea probed around his personal life, work life, social life, and then his relationship with Jesus. Adam had quick answers for everything except that.

"Uhmm, Adam? Where is Jesus?"

"Huh, what do you mean where is Jesus?"

"Exactly. I haven't heard you talk about Him."

The Holy Spirit was working through Andrea like a skilled surgeon going after cancer.

"Well Andrea…I feel kinda dry. I guess that's how some people put it… My prayers are few and far between and not very strong. I don't go to church like I used to either."

"Enough with this Adam – who are you mad at?" Andrea's question and determined look were meant to strike a nerve. One thing Andrea knew for certain was that Adam was good with words and could sweet talk her right into believing he was okay after only a few minutes of her encouraging words and a pat on the back. But not today.

"Shirley Windsor!!" Adam spewed it out almost unconsciously. "I hate her and I will never forgive her!"

The air was thick, the silence was deafening, and God was just getting warmed up.

"Well Adam, there is your problem. The Holy Spirit is convicting you of carrying a grudge."

Adam just sat and stared at Andrea. He wanted to run, like he always did, but he couldn't move. Andrea gave him a few minutes to absorb what she said before going on.

"Adam, because you refuse to forgive Shirley you are allowing her to continue to control and abuse you. And as long as you choose this, she always will. The reason you're so uncomfortable is because you are a Christian and anger, resentment, and unforgiveness doesn't fit you. It's like wearing around a pair of shoes one size too small – eventually they have to come off."

"Adam, we are commanded in God's word to forgive, not because God is a taskmaster but because He loves us. He knows how damaging hate is to the human spirit. In fact you're a perfect example. Look what has happened between you and Jesus, and just like cancer it won't stop there. It will lea... didn't say *might* – it *will* lead to the destruction of your whole life!"

Andrea's words were piercing and full of love.

This wasn't the time for a soft rebuke – Adam's life was at stake.

"But Andrea, I just don't know how…I can't find the strength."

"Adam, God knows that too. Do you remember in John chapter 5, Jesus performed His third miracle? Remember the man who laid there waiting for the water to be stirred by the angel? In fact he was paralyzed for what…38 years? What did Jesus ask him?"

"Ummm…"

"I'll tell you. Jesus asked the man, 'Do you want to get well?'"

"See Adam, the first step is to admit that you want to be well. Jesus didn't ask the man to go the the water while He stood back and watched. When the man admitted he wanted to be well, in verse 7, Jesus told him to 'get up, pick up your bedroll and walk!'"

"Jesus didn't tell the man to make himself well. Jesus isn't telling you that you have to forgive Shirley by yourself either. He is the healer, when we ask Him to be."

"What God wants to do is heal you. Not that the memories won't be there but the pain will be gone."

"Adam…look at me…Jesus loves you, and He hasn't gone anywhere. He is waiting for you to make the decision for yourself."

You could have heard a pin drop in that restaurant, and not only there, but in heaven as well. Legions of angels waiting, wondering, "Will he do it? Will he ask the master?" Some angels were glancing back and forth between Adam and Jesus. Was Adam twitching? Was Jesus giving a sign…a smile to indicate the outcome? The tension was building. Adam was searching and everyone was waiting.

"Andrea, I want to forgive Shirley Windsor."

The sun burst through the clouds, the angels were cheering throughout eternity. Andrea bowed her head and thanked the Lord.

• • • • •

Adam looked down to his wrist to check the time. "6am…I'd better get ready. I told Chaplain Smith that I would be at the prison by 8am."

If only Adam could see the anticipation and excitement brewing in the heavenlies. They'd been waiting for this day since Adam had gone home to visit his family.

The 34 mile drive to Joliet was not going to be a problem this early on a Sunday morning. In fact, with the roads being clear he could probably get there in 40-45 minutes.

Adam arrived at the main compound parking lot at 7:45am. With a few minutes to spare Adam paused and bowed his head to pray.

"Jesus, first I thank You for Your love and kindness. Thank You for rescuing me from anger and resentment. Lord, I need You to strengthen me today. I am here to let Shirley Windsor know that I've forgiven her because You have shown me how important forgiveness is. Lord, she really is my mother. Somewhere inside of me there must be a flame of love for her. No matter what she says or does I want to forgive and love her. In Your name I pray. Amen."

With that settled Adam made his way to the main visitor's entrance. There to greet him was Chaplain Smith.

Adam and the Chaplain spoke for a few minutes. The Chaplain confirmed that Shirley had attended some Bible studies, as recorded by the volunteer's attendance sheets.

"Adam, I know what is on your heart, son, and I am thankful that you want to forgive. But please remember that prison is a hard place. I have not spoken to Ms. Windsor about you, your visit, or to find out if she is a Christian even. So just know that the forgiveness is for your healing, not hers. Again, no matter what, you should look to the Lord for your peace."

"Yes sir, Chaplain Smith. I understand."

"By the way, you can call me Bill."

"Yes sir, Bill."

Adam was given a locker to put his wallet in and given all the rules concerning contact, the exchange of items, the vending machines, where to sit, and so on. Then he went through the mental detector.

The visit was a special visit, set up through the

Chaplain's office. When Shirley got the call to get ready for a visit she was floored. No one had ever visited Shirley Windsor in the 10 years she had been there.

"What??... Tracy! Hey, did the C.O. call my name for a visit?"

"Yeah, I think so. Go check it out!"

"Excuse me, C.O., did you call my name, Windsor, Shirley?"

"Yes I did. Get ready and I'll call you out."

"Yes ma'am!"

Shirley scrambled quickly to brush her teeth, comb her hair and put on a freshly ironed pair of blues – blue jeans and a scrub-type short sleeve shirt.

Shirley made her way to the visiting gallery by following some of her friends who had regular Sunday visits.

After going through the trap doors and the cursory pat down, Shirley cleared the metal detector and began to scan the crowd. "Who could it be?" she wondered.

There he was…fifth table back, by the ladies public bathroom. She promised she would never forget what Adam looked like.

Shirley eased her way up to the table. Adam noticed the woman approaching. Her hair was different, being collar length, and she had quite a few more miles worn on her face but he knew it was his mother.

"Adam? Is it really you?"

"Yes mom, it is."

With a brief hug both were nervous and uncertain as to what to say next.

Adam took the lead, "Mom, I'm sure you have a ton of questions but...well, I guess I do too...but before all that I need to tell you something. That's why I came here today."

"Okay Adam, I'll listen."

"Well, I was very mad at you for a long, long time. Even enraged at you for the way you treated Tina and I, and the fact that I didn't do anything to deserve that treatment. It wasn't my fault that dad left, and I didn't make you an alcoholic or a prostitute. I was just a child. I depended on you but you weren't there. I had to work to earn extra money instead of playing with friends. You left many scars on my emotions, and my life...Well, by God's grace I have been forgiven of all my sins against Him. And by God's grace, who is strengthening me now, I want to let you know that I have forgiven you, so that you too can find healing. I don't hold anything against you anymore."

Shirley sat there with tears falling down her face. Her hands were trembling as she reached out to take Adam's hands, "Thank you. Thank you so much."

Looking up toward heaven Shirley thanked Jesus for His mercy, and for allowing her to see her son.

"Adam, I have been praying every day for five years that God would give me the opportunity to tell you how sorry I am and ask for your forgiveness. Five years ago God rescued me and forgave me. Even though I am locked up I am free on the inside and no one can take that away."

The rest of the day was spent visiting and sharing stories of the last ten years. Adam and Shirley cried together, laughed together, and praised God for His boundless love and His great mercy.

Shirley Windsor never left the Illinois Prison for Women. She died of cancer a year and a half later – only six months from her release date. Adam was comforted in knowing that God was in charge and that He had given Adam and his mom a year and a half of joy together.

In Shirley's memory Adam and his church started a visitation and Bible ministry at the Cook County Women's Detainment Center and at the Illinois Prison for Women. Each Christmas Adam, along with his church, the Brown and Brown Agency, and many of its employees and clients share in giving special gifts. Each inmate gets two grocery sacks full of goodies to take back to her cell.

In the near future Adam hopes that through God's blessing he can open a full transformation center for women in crisis and those being released from jail or prison.

A Note from the Author

Whether you are reading this before purchasing the book or after reading it I encourage you to meditate on the goodness of God as the reason Adam's life turned out the way it did.

You see, it wasn't Adam's intelligence, or even his determination that caused the healing to take place in his life and that of his mother's. Adam was not anyone special in society's eyes. He wasn't extra smart or gifted. The difference in the outcome of his story from those of other tragic stories is that he trusted Jesus to change him and his mother.

The names and actual abuses have been altered, but the pain none the less is real. I am speaking to you from the very core of whom I was and who I have become.

I recognized in my life the pain and suffering that people go through - especially that of abused and neglected children - as horrific and catastrophic on every level. I wanted this story to prove to anyone who is willing to seek the Lord Jesus Christ for restoration that He is faithful and true to His word. He will come and make His home in them and change their lives for the good. His plan is not for harm but to give them hope and a future.

One of the greatest fears of those who have been abused is being hurt again. The damage from the abuse is due to the repeated nature of the abuse and the relentless pursuit of the abuser to somehow lash out all their anger and hurts on an innocent person. The pain and damage is real and has long lasting, and often tragic results. Many of those abused then become abusers themselves causing the cycle to repeat, even to many generations.

I am so glad to report to you that it doesn't have to be this way. Jesus is the answer to all of life's issues! I am able to write this story as a result of the healing in my life. Please understand that it wasn't a program, a pill, a doctor, a 12 step group, or any other man-made cure that brought about this depth of change in my life. It was Jesus, and Him alone, that radically changed my pain into praising, my sorrow for singing His praises, and the rage for relief.

I carried years of bitter hate to the point of even wanting to murder my abusers. I lashed out on every one in my life in the most cruel and insensitive ways. I tormented myself with doubting statements of despair, and abused my body and mind with alcohol and drugs from 14 to 43 years of age. I even did my share of jail and prison time.

As a result of the mercy and love of God toward

me, an angry bitter person, I am able to tell you God is real and has a plan for your life. I am healed through and through - on every level of my life. Spiritually, physically, emotionally, and mentally I have been made whole!

In addition to that the Lord has blessed me with a wife who loves Jesus with all her heart. Jackie is a tremendous life partner and I am so grateful to share my life with her.

May God richly bless you.
Robert Saunders

About the Author

Robert Saunders born in a small town in central Illinois in the mid 60's, learned through practical life application that "hard work never killed anyone". After getting a small taste of sales success in his teen years pursued a career in the sales industry. As is common with many in sales, he strived day in and day out to gain greater success, even if that meant relationships were torn apart by travelling and long days away from home.

After a dramatic encounter with Jesus today Robert is only after one thing: That the world will come to Jesus Christ as Lord and Savior and have their lives transformed.

Robert is married to his beautiful wife Jackie, and they live in Castalian Springs, TN. Both Robert and Jackie love to serve Jesus by serving others.